VARSITY BLUES

VARSITY BLUES

Jon Baker

POCKET BOOKS

New York London Toronto Sydney Tokyo Singapore

An *Original* Publication of MTV Books/Pocket Books

POCKET BOOKS, a division of Simon & Schuster Inc.
1230 Avenue of the Americas, New York, NY 10020

ISBN: 0-671-03568-1

First MTV Books/Pocket Books printing January 1999

10 9 8 7 6 5 4 3 2

Printed in the U.S.A.

VARSITY BLUES

1

I sat on my bed, my hair still wet from the shower, staring at the decade old snapshot I'd nabbed from my trophy shelf. There I was, Jonathan Moxon—Mox to most folks—aged seven or eight, grinning in an oversized blue-on-blue football jersey. My hair, which is now light brown and wavy, was still blond. My strong-jawed, square face was softer in childhood. My buds grinned out at me from the photo, too. Lance Harbor, Tweeder, Billy Bob—already busting the seams of his peewee league uniform. Our faces were streaked with dirt. We squinted into the camera in the bright Texas sun. We looked like we were having fun.

Off camera, on the sidelines, our fathers

would have been coaching our practice. They wouldn't have been wearing our carefree smiles. They knew. We didn't. Yet.

See, in America, we have laws against killing and stealing and it's just accepted that as a member of American society, you will live by these laws. In West Canaan, Texas, there is another society that has its own laws and we just accept them with no consent. Football is a way of life. Mind you, this is Texas where people still sell God door-to-door, but the phenomenon of high-school football is absolutely sacred. As a boy growing up in West Canaan, Texas, you never questioned the sanctity of high-school football. You just listened to what the coaches said and tried as best you could to win. Win at all costs.

"Think you'll play tonight?" My little trip down memory lane was intercepted by my eleven-year-old brother, Kyle. I glanced over at him. He had a huge wooden cross strapped to his back, and his hands were tied to the crossbeam at the wrists. A brown-haired, crew-cut, smurf-faced Jesus Christ right in my very own bedroom. I didn't blink. I was used to my kid brother's little peculiarities.

"Do I ever play?" I asked him.

"No, but—"

"Lance is the best quarterback in three counties," I said. "Why would we want anyone but him to play?" It was a fact. I wasn't feeling sorry for myself. Football was about winning. End of sentence. I was the second-string quarterback. I was good. At least, I thought so. But Lance was West Canaan High's starting Q.B. Lance was the man. Lance could win.

"Well, maybe if you guys are running up the score . . ." Kyle said, half-heartedly.

I left the old photo on my bed and started walking out of the room. It wasn't gonna happen. I wasn't gonna see any playing time. No matter what the score.

"Or if Lance gets hurt and—"

I turned and tackled Kyle to the ground. Strapped to that cross, he crashed to the carpet like a dead man. "Don't even think about Lance going down," I ordered him. I felt the fear even saying it. "That'd be a disaster." I wasn't sure which thought was scarier—that West Canaan would lose without Lance, or that they'd lose with me as the substitute quarterback. Besides, Lance Harbor was my best friend. I eased up on Kyle. "As a man of the cross, or, in your situation, a man *on* the cross, I ask you to pray for the health of Lance Harbor."

I left Kyle crucified on the floor, and headed downstairs to breakfast.

* * *

3

I had to zigzag like I was scrambling on the football field to avoid Mom as she flew around the kitchen pouring and mixing and frying everything in target range. She was a breakfast warrior in a helmet of curlers, waiting on her general—that general being Dad, sitting in his designated spot at the table, eating eggs and home fries and reading the sports section. His navy tie with the light blue footballs was thrown over one shoulder to avoid damage from the sunnyside ups. He looked up at me as I grabbed a biscuit off the table.

"Son, did you pray for playing time?" he asked.

"I just spoke to Jesus upstairs," I answered.

"Who?"

"The crucified eleven-year-old living in my room."

Mom stopped frying for a second. "Is Kyle strapped to that cross again?" she said, shaking her head slightly.

"Yup," I said. I grabbed a fork and scarfed a few bites of egg directly from the pan on the stove.

"Kyle!" Dad roared. "Why is he so difficult?" he said to Mom, sounding as if maybe it was somehow her fault.

Kyle came into the kitchen, turning sideways to get through the doorframe. He went straight for the biscuits, too, but with that cross on, he had to tilt his whole body and do this wriggle-fingered deal to snag one. Dad glared at him.

"Kyle! What is it with the cross?"

I could see Kyle trying to figure out how he was going to get that biscuit into his mouth, when he couldn't bend his arm. "I am preparing to die for all of man's sins," he recited.

Mom flashed Dad a feeble little what-can-you-do smile. "That's sweet, honey," she said to Kyle. She went back to her frying.

"I want it off, now!" Dad thundered. "How do you expect your brother to concentrate on football with you running around with this whole deal strapped to your back?"

Kyle took a backwards step, retreating from Dad's anger. I felt bad for him. "Dad, he's just . . ." Just what? Just not your average red-blooded, football-playing eleven-year-old. And power to you, little dude, I thought. That wasn't so easy around West Canaan.

"Enough!" Dad said tightly. "I'm serious. We all need to concentrate on tonight's game." I felt the Pre-game Lecture coming on.

I was saved by the doorbell. "Might be Billy Bob," I said, taking my cue to exit.

I pulled open the door to find a strange man in a blue polyester suit and blue tie, smiling beatifically at me. In one hand he held a Bible.

"Hey, good morning, I'd love to tell you the good news about my best friend, Jesus Christ!" The smile never left his face as he talked.

Speaking of Jesus, Jesus, was I surrounded by nut jobs.

"Kyle! Someone for you!" I shouted.

The nasal blare of a car horn playing "Yellow Rose of Texas" distracted me from our born-again visitor. Billy Bob's beat-up blue pickup, his jersey number—69—painted on the cab door, idled at the end of my driveway in the wan, early morning light.

Kyle appeared next to me, his outstretched arms filling the doorway. Our visitor's smile slipped only for a moment. "Uh, I'd love to tell you the good news about my best friend, Jesus Christ," he repeated for my brother's benefit.

"Well, it's not working for me," Kyle said somberly. "The dude got stapled to a stick in his underwear. I just don't think I can back him anymore." He managed to shrug a wrist loose from bondage. Then he yanked free the other. The cross went crashing to the floor behind him.

I heard Dad coming up in back of us. "Am I the only one who cares about football in this house?"

I stepped out the door, edging around the smiling man in blue. Kyle slammed the door behind me, in our visitor's face. Like I said, nut jobs. I was glad to be outta there this morning. I crossed the lawn to Billy Bob's truck. Billy Bob, all three hundred something balloon-shaped pounds of him, was wedged into the driver's seat, howling like a Coyote. That's us. The West Canaan Coyotes. Billy Bob's plug-shaped head was crowned by a dark brown fade. In the flatbed of the truck, Wendell McReady was studying from his bio textbook. Wendell is 185 lean, muscle-bound pounds of ebony-skinned power, the fastest, strongest high-school running back this side of the Rio Grande. West Canaan kinda made him a deal he couldn't refuse, moving his family from a modest house in the next town over to a much sweeter deal here. Of course, that kind of thing's not really legit. It's supposed to be some kind of Coyotes's secret, but Wendell's a critical part of our team, and my pal besides, so I'm glad we got him.

I had my hand raised to greet him, when all of a sudden, Billy Bob was taking off—backing out of the driveway, passenger door wide open, before I'd even reached the truck. "Mox!" he yelled, laughing insanely. "You skinny ass bitch! Let's roll!" And he rolled. Right over the hedges that separated our driveway from the Morris's next door. I turned it on, sprinting to catch up to the moving truck. Billy Bob floored the gas. I gave it everything I had. I felt the burn in my legs.

"C'mon, Mox, earn it!" Billy Bob guffawed. Damn that fat porker, I thought, as I took a flying leap at the open door and managed to get a handhold. I pulled myself into the passenger seat and came face-to-face with . . . a fat porker. A *real* fat porker. And I'm not talking names for Billy Bob, either. A pink and brown, full-grown pig shared the passenger side of the cab with me. I panted, catching my breath. The pig snorted back at me.

"Bacon, hop in the flatbed," Billy Bob said.

The pig obediently hustled his huge, blub-bery self through the rear window of the cab and into the flatbed with Wendell.

Through the window, I watched Wendell jump to his feet and away from Bacon. He brushed an imaginary smudge from his blue and snow-white Reebok sweatpants. To match his Reebok sneakers. And his Reebok warm-up jacket that he wore over his Coyotes jersey. And his Reebok reading glasses. "I'm tellin' you, Billy Bob. This swine fucks up my new suit and he's road ham."

"Sorry, Wendell. Just kick him off," Billy Bob said.

"I'm serious. I'll toss your pig ass on the street," Wendell told Bacon.

Billy Bob grabbed a paper bag off the dash, riffled around in it and pulled out a pancake, a jar of peanut butter and a knife. Steering with his knees, he slathered the peanut butter on the rubbery pancake. He folded the whole thing in half and stuffed it into his mouth. I watched in awe. He made some exaggerated chewing motions, a gargantuan swallow, and managed to get the thing down in a few gulps. He pulled an industrial-sized bottle of maple syrup from between his oversized thighs, and washed his snack down. I guess it's a talent. Then he reached back and gave Bacon a light slap on the rear. "God, I love that dawg," he said, letting out an impressive belch.

"I think it's a pig," I said mildly.

"Yeah," Billy Bob agreed genially. He stepped on the gas and the truck powered forward. Back in the flatbed, Wendell held on to the side of the truck. Bacon just fell over with a loud, dull thud. Billy Bob let out another howl. You could see the sugar rush kicking in. Just another morning in West Canaan.

West Canaan, Texas. Population 9,379. Home of Kilmer's Coyotes. That's what the football-shaped sign out on Route 1 reads. Kilmer is Coach Kilmer. Coach Bud Kilmer, Sir. But I'm getting ahead of myself. You'll meet him soon enough. Can't get away from him in West Canaan.

Billy Bob roared past the sign. He steered with his elbows and knees, scarfing more p.b. pancake roll-ups, and swigging maple syrup like a cold Bud on a hot day. A dark green mini-van coming in the opposite direction wove over the line, a tire crossing into our lane. Billy Bob jerked the steering wheel with his thigh and missed the van by an inch.

In the back of the truck, Wendell was unfazed. He was studying his textbook again while Bacon poked his head over the edge of the flatbed, lapping up air like a dog at his feeding bowl. Billy Bob took a turn off Route 1, and sped through a neighborhood of wide, tree-lined streets and sprawling houses. Some of them were painted blue with light blue trim, our team colors. The sun was just starting to brighten their roofs and glint off their big bay windows. A blue Coyote banner stretched across a street, from one telephone pole to another. Billy Bob zoomed under it, squealed around a corner, and came to an abrupt stop. I heard the loud, dull thud. Bacon was down again.

We were stopped in front of Lance Harbor's blue-on-blue three-story home. It was bigger than my house, with a flower bed in front of the neat porch and high hedges marking the prop-erty lines. But what really made it stand out was the huge sign on the manicured front lawn.

No—scratch that. It wasn't even a sign. It was a billboard. A mammoth, highway-sized billboard that blocked a major part of the house from view. Lance was immortalized on it, throwing a perfect pass, larger than life. HOME OF LANCE HARBOR, ALL TEXAS QUARTERBACK, the sign said.

And then Lance appeared in the flesh, the real, live, in-person Lance Harbor, emerging onto his doorstep, perfect biceps rippling under his football jersey, perfect, sun-kissed blond hair framing a chiseled face . . . you know, your basic Greek God—or star Texas quarterback. Same thing, right?

Colette Harbor, his stepmother, came out behind him, stooping to retrieve the newspaper at their door. She stood again, smoothing her silk bathrobe with her free hand. The robe was barely there—short enough to give us a look at her really hot body. Lance's stepmom had graduated from New Canaan High about ten years ago, and she still looked like the head cheerleader she'd been back then. Slender but curvy. Long, tawny legs. Cascades of blond hair. Okay, I was staring. Billy Bob was staring. Drooling.

Mrs. Harbor—Colette—looked over at us, tossed her mane of hair, and waved smoothly. She was joined by Lance's balding, not-nearly-so-perfect Dad, who affixed his right hand to his wife's ass—its permanent resting place in this world.

" 'Member when Lance's stepmom . . . uh . . . Colette was a cheerleader . . ." Billy Bob said, still ogling.

"Yeah?" I said.

"And we used to crawl under the bleachers to look up . . . Colette's skirt and she was never wearing any—"

"Billy Bob!" I shouted, startling him back down to Earth.

Billy Bob gave his head a shake, blinked, and looked over at Lance, who sauntered toward the truck. Billy Bob opened his door and hopped out, standing at attention as Lance approached. "You need anything, big guy, you let me know," he greeted Lance.

Lance grabbed Billy Bob in a rough hug. Lance does a lot of hugging. You know—he loves life, loves his friends. Everything is sincerely sunny in Lance Harbor's universe. And why shouldn't it be? He's the star quarterback, and this is Texas.

"I love you, my brother," Lance told Billy Bob. "I had a beautiful dream last night."

Billy Bob smiled as if he'd been blessed by the Pope, and hustled back into the driver's seat. Lance hopped into the flatbed with Wendell. "Wendell, I love you, my brother. I am a visionary," Lance added.

Up in the cab, I raised a silent eyebrow. Lance

was my best friend. But a visionary? Well, in West Canaan, Lance Harbor can be whoever he wants . . .

Next stop was the humble home of Chardy Tweeder. And I do mean humble. It was the black sheep on the block, the lawn like a bad haircut, the two basement windows broken and boarded up with dirty sheets of plywood. No billboard at this casa humilde. Billy Bob didn't get out and stand at attention. He barely even slowed down as Tweeder ran howling through the deep grass in front of his house and dove headfirst into the flatbed. Billy Bob peeled away from the curb, visions of Colette Harbor still dancing in his head.

How did I know? Trust me. I've known Billy Bob forever. Besides, he couldn't stop talking about her.

"She's the perfect wife for me, Mox, I would love Colette," he said, stuffing his lovelorn face with another pancake and peanut butter. "I would," he mumbled, mouth full to bursting.

"That would make you Lance's stepdad," I reminded him.

Billy Bob chewed and swallowed. "I'd love him, too," he said. He already did.

Suddenly, through the rear window of the cab, the moon was rising—as in the round, muscular ass that had pushed its way through the window and wedged itself between me and Billy Bob, like a third head joining our conversation. Tweeder's butt sported a blue tattoo of a West Canaan Coyote.

Billy Bob and I were silent for a moment. Then the ass disappeared. A second later, it was replaced by Tweeder's blue-eyed, strong-boned face, his mouth going a mile a minute as he sing-songed at us. "Good *mooning*, boys! Good *mooning*. I've been up since the *crack* of dawn and I had to *ass* you something . . ."

"Try to calm down, Tweeder," I said. "Did you take the right medication today?"

Tweeder didn't stop to take a breath. "What's up with Kira Anne Bailes?" he plowed on.

"Darcy's friend?" Billy Bob asked.

Tweeder's eyes gleamed. Definitely deranged. "She's got that look, like, I just fell out the I'm-gonna-suck-yer-dick tree and hit every branch on the way down!" Poor Tweetie was one small step away from foaming at the mouth.

"You got to relax, Tweet. Focus," I said gently.

But Tweeder just turned up the volume. "I can't! I gotta get some tonight. It's critical. This pig's lookin' good t' me right now. Hump, hump, hump! That's what I'm all about!"

Right, Tweeder. Meanwhile, I could hear Lance orating like a preacher back there.

"I drifted off to sleep, and I had a dream!" he

proclaimed to Wendell, his voice swelling with mysticism and power.

"Oh yeah, brother, a dream. I hear you," Wendell echoed back. They faced each other, doing their call and response, solidarity forever and all that.

"Can I hug you?" Lance asked. As I said, Lance had this thing about hugging everyone.

I wondered what he'd dreamed about. Fame? Fortune? Winning tonight's game? Probably. I glanced through the cab window at him and Wendell. How had I wound up on this alien planet? The only thing that marked me as one of their species was the blue game jerseys we were all wearing, with our names and numbers on them.

Billy Bob finished his Herculean breakfast as we wheeled through town and peeled up the access road to West Canaan High. Billy Bob had to slow down as we neared the players' parking lot. Either that or take out some of our loyal fans who swarmed across the road on the way to the morning pep rally in the gym. It was a sea of light blue on blue. The fiercest fans had gone further than mere blue clothing. Blue nail polish, blue hair, even blue greasepaint all over some of their faces.

Tweeder hooted and hollered, calling attention to the truck so we could revel in our star status. Lance smiled down upon the little people, waving like the young JFK in his motorcade. A towering marquee on the lawn of school read COYOTES FRIDAY NIGHT—HOME VS. BINGVILLE. Nearby stood a life-sized statue of the coach—that's Coach, Sir, to you—hands on hips, looking sternly out across his turf, capable of instilling fear and awe in the hearts of big, strong guys who oughta know better. But I'm getting ahead of myself again . . .

2

It was pure pandemonium in the gym. The entire school was packed in there, a writhing, tsunami-swept ocean of crazed football fans. The deafening noise rose to the high ceilings. Not even the cheering squad, in action on the far side of the gym, could be heard clearly in all the chaos. Our starting offense—our pantheon of the eleven major West Canaan High School gods—stood on a riser set up along the window-side wall, sunlight streaming in behind them to illuminate them for the masses. Coach Kilmer stood in front of them, hands on hips, looking sternly out across his turf. His deep-set blue eyes and narrow mouth were set in a steely expression. His brown hair was graying at the temples, making him look even more severe. The rest of the team—us forty minor gods—flanked the guys on the riser like bridesmaids around a bride.

I was jostled by the crowd as they surged forward to get closer to the starting players. Two babe-a-licious young things—freshmen or sophomores, from the looks of them—rushed the riser and got up front and center near Lance, pulling at his jersey to get his attention.

Lance looked down at them and smiled magnanimously. "Lance!" squealed one of them, an auburn-haired, fresh-faced nymphet in a blue, pleated mini. "Lance, can I have your autograph?" She held a black magic marker out like a ceremonial offering, hoisting her skirt up to reveal a perfectly toned, round perky cheek on which Lance could ink his John Hancock.

Lance blushed—ever the perfect gentleman—but stepped down off his pedestal to oblige her. As he capped the marker and handed it back to her, the other girl, a small, curly-headed blonde, shoved her aside. "You're Lance Harbor!" she said, big blue eyes open wide with excitement. "And I'm . . . I'm . . . I can't remember who I am! Wait! This is my moment. I'm . . . my name is . . . wait!"

But her moment was over as the crowd surged forward and she was pounded to the ground. Lance did a quick retreat to his place on the riser.

At a microphone in front of the riser stood a short, slight, forlorn figure, tapping the mike and trying to call the crowd to order. "Attention! Attention, people," he recited in vain. This was our principal, Hamilton Boggs—Ham to most of us. "Please, people, quiet! C'mon, hands on heads, hands on heads." Ham placed his hands on his bald pate like a first-grade teacher, but the noise didn't subside. A football went whizzing by him. He gave an audible sigh. "Please welcome Coach Kilmer!" he announced.

The coach stepped over to the mike. The noise level swelled to its absolute maximum. But with one raise of Kilmer's hand—the dictator's salute—the gym fell as silent as a church. He dropped his hand. "Tonight we play Bingville," he broadcast to his minions. "Tonight we beat Bingville." It was a proclamation, an order, a fact. It had to happen. The coach had spoken.

He raised his hand again. The crowd roared to show they were with him all the way. When he dropped his hand, total silence. "In my thirty-five years as coach at West Canaan, I have had the honor of coaching some great individuals," he began. "Many of the great men of this community started out as boys on my football team. I have brought twenty-two district championships and two state titles to West Canaan and this year, God willing, I will bring number twenty-three."

His hand went up. Near riot-level noise punctured the stuffy air in the gym. Hand down. Not a sound. "I present to you my starting offense, led by quarterback Lance Harbor."

The crowd went berserk. The shrieks of the female population of West Canaan added a high, reverb-like screech to the cacophony. Lance stepped off the riser and took the mike. He grinned confidently. He was strong, he was invincible, he was . . . Our Hero. "I was layin' in bed last night," he told the crowd. Even more ecstatic cries from the ladies at the thought of our own Lance Harbor in bed. "And I drifted off to sleep and I had a dream that we're beating Bingville fourteen to three."

The fans roared at Lance's mighty prediction.

"And I woke up kinda sad," Lance said. The roar mutated into an empathetic *Ohhh*. No one wanted our star quarterback to be sad. "But then I cheered up when I realized it was only a dream, cuz I know we'll beat Bingville by way more than that!" Lance delivered the punchline with appropriate triumph.

The kids in the gym cheered insanely. Lance smiled modestly, the humble god before his followers. He was good. I give him that. You couldn't find a better role model. And I mean, the guy's my bud. Has been all my life.

But there was a certain other person in his family who I'd gotten even more attached to recently. I scanned the crowd for that certain person. Julie . . . Jules. I caught sight of her standing cool and unruffled amidst the fanatics. A year younger than Lance, she had a thick, straight, shiny mane of brown hair just past her shoulders, a pretty, heart-shaped face with big hazel eyes and a beauty mark on her cheek, a kissably full mouth, and a lean, athletic body. She was beautiful in a fresh, natural way. And she had a great smile. When she saw that I'd found her, she flashed that smile at me and shook her head at the hysteria.

I wandered away from the riser and headed over to her. No one was gonna miss me. Not with Lance up there. "Kilmer really gets off on this," I greeted her. "Look, he offers your brother to the masses like a god." Lance waved to the crowd like a newly crowned Miss America.

Julie shrugged. "He's the quarterback."

"Yeah, like I said, he's their god," I repeated.

A five-foot-five-inch package of Pammie Lee Anderson–brand sex-appeal came over to us and caught the last sentence of our conversation. This was Darcy Sears, head cheerleader and

Lance's girlfriend. I'd known Darcy since elementary school, but there was nothing childlike about the siren call that oozed from every barely dressed cell of her body. Darcy was hot, and she flaunted it. And it was hard for most of us in the male species not to appreciate that.

"He's *my* god," she said, putting a spin on my words. "Just think, Jules, if I marry Lance you and I will be sisters."

"Just think, Darcy, you and my stepmom could do cheerleading routines around the house," Julie answered with sugary sarcasm. She pumped her fist in the air.

I swallowed my laugh. I could see Darcy was insulted. But before she and Jules could face off, the crowd went into the famous West Canaan Coyote Call. The Coyote Call sounds like four hundred teenagers howling like dogs because it is four hundred teenagers howling like dogs. Eardrum damage level, on the real. I grabbed Julie's hand and pushed through the crowd, leading her away from the sound and the fury.

We burst out of the heavy, swinging doors, and into the relative tranquillity of the hallway. The Coyote Call was only a dull roar out here.

"Thank you," Julie said. "I had to get outta there." She ran her hands through her brown hair as if putting herself back in order after toughing out the pep rally. I don't know how

Julie managed to escape a critical case of football fever growing up in West Canaan. Especially in the Harbor household. Maybe it was that Lance had gotten all the football genes, and left his sister with none. Or maybe it was because as a girl, she was never a contender. Maybe all the focus on Lance, Lance, Lance had led her to wage her own personal revolution. Or maybe it was that she was smart enough to stop and look around her and realize that football couldn't possibly be the only thing on the planet. Don't get me wrong. I think football is a great game. Or it can be. But the way we did it in West Canaan made it more like a religious cult. "Tell me this insanity is over in a coupla weeks," Julie pleaded.

"It is," I assured her. "Five more games. No more football and no more Kilmer." I felt a breeze of relief, too. "And if I get into Brown, no more West Canaan." I was New England bound. At least I hoped I was. Providence, R.I.—halfway between the cities of Boston and New York. Yeah, I had heard all about the urban legends there, but I didn't think that football was quite so high on the mythical scale in those parts.

"And no more games on Friday nights . . ." Julie added. She moved in close to me. I could smell her delicate perfume mixing with the sweetness of her shampoo. Her face was turned up to mine. Her brown eyes shone.

"You don't like football on Friday nights?" I asked softly. It wasn't the game I was really asking about. I knew how Jules felt. I was really asking about the post-game—as in me and Jules finding somewhere to celebrate, just the two of us.

"I like trains better," Julie whispered back, smiling sweetly.

Okay, we were on the same page here. The cove under the railroad bridge was an excellent place for getting cozy. "You wanna watch trains tonight?" I asked her.

"I'll watch trains with you anytime," she said. She leaned in and gave me a long, sweet kiss. Her lips were soft and moist. Our bodies pressed together. The roar of the Coyote Call faded into the background.

Game time. I drove the Moxmobile—my blue '98 Delta—through town on the way to the stadium, watching store owners lock up tight. It was as if a hurricane was due to blow through. Which I guess it basically was. Hurricane Football. The neon-lettered sign over the Cineplex went dark as I rolled by. The shops on Main were dim, metal gates pulled down over the pharmacy door and windows, the ovens off at Gibson's Bakery. On the corner of Main and

Orange, even Murray's Bar was closing down for a few, Murray himself shooing two barflies out the door, bottles in hand.

The drunks clinked their Buds and stumbled down the street, probably toasting to the success of the Coyotes. I rounded a corner and a police cruiser drove past. I got a glimpse of Sheriff Bigelow, who'd traded in his regulation white cowboy hat for a Kilmer's Coyotes cap.

I pulled out onto Route 1 and passed the mall. Empty. Walmart's was dark and locked, too, of course. Of course, because Lance and Julie's dad is the manager. Right about now, he and Colette and Jules would be piling into their van, carrying seat cushions and caps, T-shirts, blankets and pennants—all light blue on blue, all decorated with a howling Coyote, all from Walmart's, and available for a special, low, low price. Joe Harbor would be so excited about his merchandise and his son and the whole nine yards—literally—that he'd even forget to attach his right hand to his wife's ass from time to time.

Julie would just be along for the ride. Attendance at the game was mandatory. But she didn't have to like it.

And my dad? Down at the sewage plant, he'd have already sent his men home, and was more than likely struggling without success to get into his ancient Coyotes jersey.

On the real? Maybe I felt just a little bit left out.

I pulled into the parking lot of the Bud Kilmer Stadium. Yeah. Our stadium's named after Coach Kilmer. Like in some towns they name their important structures after a president or a local war hero . . .

The tailgate party was in high gear. Kids chugging brewskis, going through sixers like this was their last night on Earth. Folks pumping tunes out of their car stereos, the smell of crisped meat greeting my nostrils as people barbecued dogs and burgers on grills they'd set up right in the parking lot. A knot of kids in blue exchanged angry words with the crimson-clothed opposition. The taunts escalated and I saw someone throw the first punch.

I didn't stick around for the melee. I drove on toward the players' lot. I could see people streaming into the stadium—old and young, families, couples, groups of friends. The circular, open-aired building was bathed in fierce white light streaming from mammoth light towers. The air was charged.

As I hopped out of the Moxmobile and locked my door, fans called out to me, wishing me good luck. I waved my thanks. Even though it was up to Lance and not me.

Inside the locker room, it was quieter than it was outside. The warriors prepared for battle in focused silence. Taping ankles and wrists. Drawing charcoal streaks under their eyes—our own brand of war paint. Strapping on pads. The occasional touching to the lips of some charm or talisman or girlfriend's photo. Rituals, performed intently, quietly.

Well, mostly quietly. Then there was Billy Bob, who couldn't resist the urge to punch his meaty fist into his locker. He grabbed me as I walked past him.

"I love this shit," he growled, raging animal hormones. "I gotta get it out, Mox. Gotta hurt somebody." I wrested myself from his grip. I didn't intend for me to be the somebody. But Billy Bob kept holding me in his feral gaze. "And yea though I walk through the valley of the shadow of death," he intoned, "I fear no faggots from Bingville.—"

I walked away from him. Over in the row of toilet stalls, there was audible evidence that someone was in there puking his guts out. Losing dinner. And lunch. Worshiping at the altar of the porcelain god. The hurling stopped. I heard the toilet flush. Wendell emerged, looking none the worse for the upheaval. It wasn't all that unusual for him to get his nerves out this way. All part of the game. "Every time I puke, we win," he said to me.

I patted Wendell on the back. He smiled and

returned the pat. "Stay loose, Mox. You never know when Kilmer might play you." Well, that would be kinda fun, I thought. Break up the unbearable excitement of warming the bench. But it ain't gonna happen.

Tweetie was doing this random little dance in the middle of the room. "What d'ya think of the new Tweeder touchdown dance?" he asked me as I went by. "I'm gonna call it . . ." He stopped dancing to think. That's because Tweeder has to concentrate harder than some to get his brain in gear. "I'm gonna call it the new Tweeder touchdown dance." He grinned.

I headed past the trainer's room on the way to my locker. The door was open a crack and I peered in. Lance was sitting on the table, Coach Kilmer at his side, as the trainer stuck a hypodermic needle into Lance's knee. Lance cringed, but almost imperceptibly. What was up with the needle? I didn't know anything about a bum knee.

The coach caught my eye and glared. He charged the door and slammed it in my face.

Fourth quarter. West Canaan Coyotes: 28. Bingville Bulls: 17. The home team crowd is starting to celebrate already. We're caked with mud and covered with blood. Warriors, for real. Well, they are. I'm warming the bench—my designated position—a good novel tucked inside my playbook. Kurt Vonnegut's *Slaughterhouse Five,* an awesome book about a World War II prisoner of war who comes unstuck in time. Speaking of warriors. I'd highly recommend it.

Out on the field, it was our own kind of slaughterhouse. I glanced up from my book to check out Lance, the consummate cool customer, maintaining order within the ranks of his teammates, amidst the violence. Facing third down and long, Lance dropped back to pass. A massive Bingville lineman found a hole in the pocket and went for him. I tightened reflexively as the monster head-butted into his gut. But Lance just managed to get the pass off, connecting with his wide receiver, before he was knocked to the ground. First down. I felt a wave of admiration for Lance. Awesome play.

The cheerleaders were shouting out the praises of Lance Harbor. Jumping, kicking, turning somersaults for our man. The fans in the bleachers were on their feet. In the V.I.P. section, Joe Harbor—Lance's dad—had his hands cupped to his mouth like a megaphone. But you didn't need to be able to hear him to know what he was shouting. "Attaboy, Lance! First down! All night long!"

Colette Harbor pounded her fist against the sky. She always came to games in a team jacket that said QUARTERBACK'S MOM on the back. A biological impossibility, or nearly one, but I guess "Quarterback's *Stepmom*" didn't quite cut it.

I could see Julie there with them, on her feet just to avoid a scene with her father, clapping politely.

My family was there, too, a few rows away from the Harbors. They never missed a game. They were more reserved in their cheering than the Harbors, but I guess it was even harder for them to see me on the bench the whole game than for me to be there. Kyle had lost the cross, but now he was wearing a sheetlike, saffron-colored Buddhist sarong, and sitting up there in the bleachers in lotus position. Not your average eleven-year-old's favorite pastime. I could only imagine what my father was saying to Kyle in the wake of Lance's perfect throw. "Kyle,"—I could almost hear him—"you should be takin' notes."

Maybe he thought I should be taking notes, too.

Lance set the game in motion, barking signals at the line of scrimmage. He dropped back to pass again. But this time he overthrew and missed his receiver. The home crowd moaned their collective disappointment as the errant pass sailed over our sideline and landed near me.

I eyed the pigskin, and went over to pick it up. The referee was far down the field—the same ref who'd blown a blatant pass interference call in the first quarter that should have gone our way. I pulled my arm back and heaved a perfect spiral, fifty yards easy—smack dab into the ref's gut. Not bad for a second stringer. If he'd been closer, I would have heard the *Ummph*! I grinned. That felt good. A hum of admiration went through the crowd, and I felt a jolt of pride—like maybe one one-hundredth of what Lance was feeling out there. But, hey.

I sat back down with a little smile, ready to go back to the book inside my playbook. Until I heard Joe Harbor's voice boom out to my father in the stands. "Sam, that's about the most action your boy's seen, ain't it?"

I gritted my teeth. Lance's dad had been on him like fleas on a dog ever since high school. At least that's what my mom said.

Meanwhile, Joe Harbor's boy was out there pulverizing Bingville. I saw him look toward the coach to read his signals. Without really thinking about it, I did the same. Quarterback keeper on a sweep left.

I saw Wendell break away from the huddle in frustration. He wasn't getting the ball. And after carrying it, let's see—seven times, I think, for almost 70 yards on this current drive—they should have gone to him here on first and goal. I could see why he was mad.

But Lance was just following orders and con-
centrating on the game. We were only minutes
away from winning. There was no way Bingville
could catch up. Lance rolled out an option.
Billy Bob pulled guard, trampling a path for
Lance around the right side of the field. I don't
know if it was those peanut butter pancakes or
what—Billy Bob was a bulldozer. Nobody could
stop him. He led Lance into the end zone, free
and easy.

Touchdown!

But Billy Bob was still going, going . . . gone
as he smacked straight into the goalpost.
BOOM! A wide-bodied truck smashing into a
brick wall. I saw him fall. I was on my feet and
running.

"His helmet's cracked right in half!" I heard
one of my teammates yelling.

My breath came too fast as I knelt by his side.
His eyes were closed under his cracked helmet.
I called his name, but I didn't dare touch him.
Kilmer and Assistant Coach Bates raced over.
The Coyotes gathered around. "He's de-ad! Billy
Bob's dead!" cried a meaty halfback named Ful-
son.

Our team doctor rushed over and pushed his
way through the players. He whipped out the
smelling salts and passed them under Billy
Bob's nose. Billy Bob flinched. He blinked. He

batted his eyes like a beauty contestant. Then he came to life. He reached up and pulled his helmet apart, like he was prying open the shell of a walnut. He beamed me a smile. "Ay, Mox. That was gre-at! I must've killed that Bingville dude," he said cluelessly. "Check out this helmet, man. It's a keeper, huh?"

Doc Patterson waved a couple of fingers in front of Billy Bob's face. "How many fingers, son? How many now?"

"Uh, three? One? Six?" Billy Bob kept getting it wrong.

I knew something about Billy Bob that the good doctor didn't. "Hold on," I said. "It's gotta be true or false."

"True or false?" Doc Patterson echoed uncomprehendingly.

I held three fingers up to Billy Bob's swelling head. "Billy Bob, I'm holding up some fingers, true or false?"

"True?" Billy Bob ventured.

"He's okay," I announced.

I glanced up at the scoreboard. It was West Canaan 35, Bingville 17. All we had to do was kick off and watch the clock tick down the final seconds . . . 3, 2, 1 . . . The gun went off. Jubilation in the bleachers. The mad howling of an entire town.

And the victory belonged to the Coyotes.

3

While the fans reveled and rejoiced, the players funneled back to the locker room. Dog-tired after the big win. In pain, limping. Uniforms filthy with dirt and blood. A least that was the case for most of us. Billy Bob was led off the field by a pair of trainers flanking him and nearly dragging him inside. But I was as bright and shiny as a ref's whistle.

As I entered the locker room, I felt someone behind me grab the neck of my jersey. "Mox!"

It was Coach Kilmer. Sir. "Yeah, Coach?"

Kilmer tore my playbook out of my hands. Opened it. Found my dirty little secret. His voice was low and threatening as he shook my novel at me. "If your daddy hadn't played his heart out for me, I'd cut your ass." He drilled the book across the locker room as if he were letting one fly into the end zone.

The guys iced their bruises, licked their wounds, collapsed where they fell. I sat on a bench—like I said, my designated position—keeping Lance company as he fielded congratulations.

"Way to go!"

"Great game!"

"Right on!"

Kilmer entered the room, and everyone quieted down, fast. He got right to the point. "Tonight's game ball goes to Lance Harbor."

No surprise there. He threw the ball to Lance. "Here's another one fer yer shelf," he said.

We all applauded.

Then the coach went over to Wendell, who sat on a bench icing his sore knees. He slapped Wendell on the back. "Pretty good job tonight runnin' the ball," he said. "Really not bad. How do you feel, boy?"

Wendell managed a shrug. "Beat, Coach. My knees, they—" He stopped in mid-sentence as he caught the steely look on the coach's face.

"Go on, boy. The only pain that matters is the pain you inflict," Kilmer said severely. "Never show weakness. Look at Billy Bob. He's got enough heart for all a yas."

Billy Bob, standing buck naked in the middle of the locker room, looked drunk with pride from Kilmer's special mention. Or maybe he'd started partying early.

"Let him hear it," Coach Kilmer commanded. "C'mon."

Wendell was still absorbing the coach's put down, and the oily way Kilmer made a point of calling him "boy." You could see the anger on Wendell's face.

Assistant Coach Bates began to clap. The players joined in half-heartedly. Coach Kilmer was suddenly staring me in the face. I put my hands together for Billy Bob. And he did deserve the recognition, no lie. But damn that bastard, Kilmer. Wendell deserved the recognition, too.

Kilmer turned away and I stopped clapping. "Four more games," I said to Lance, my voice low but hard.

"Hang in, man. You're doin' fine," Lance said easily. "Tweetie, dude," he whispered to Tweeder. "Got any?"

Tweeder dug into his locker. On the d.l., he slapped a vial of pain pills into Lance's palm. Lance took a surreptitious look at it. "Five hundred milligrams. Sweetness. How many?"

"Keep 'em," Tweeder said. "I got more. Fuckin' Kilmer," he added, glaring at the coach's back. "I'm getting blotto tonight."

Tweetie was speaking for everyone, no lie.

Jules and I could hear the party even before we pulled around the corner. Hear it and feel it. The music pulsated through the ground. Shook the walls of the neat, wood-framed two-story house. Kids were sprawled all over the lawn, lying in the flower beds, up in the trees. Beer flowed like the Rio Grande from a keg on the porch.

On the porch steps, we found Billy Bob and Bacon, and a slender, sweet-faced girl. Billy Bob, held on to Bacon by the collar he'd fastened around his neck. Bacon strained to get away.

"Bacon! C'mere, Bacon," he was saying, as we approached the house. He tugged on Bacon's leash with one hand, and held his big, black cowboy hat on with the other.

The girl was taking an interest in Bacon. "Boy or girl?" she wanted to know.

"What d'ya mean is he a boy or a girl?" Suddenly, Billy Bob was on his feet, hoisting the massive Bacon in the air with a grunt of muscle power. "See? Bacon's got a sausage!" he said drunkenly. "Oh, hey, Mox! Julie!" Billy Bob let Bacon back down.

We slid handshakes. Billy Bob smelled like a brewery. After we'd left him with his new friend on the porch, Julie expressed her concern. "Shouldn't Billy Bob be takin' it easy? He really banged his head tonight."

I shrugged. "He's convinced that beer's good for him." He seemed okay. I mean, Billy Bob's version of okay.

Inside, we said hi to a bunch of people. Tunes were cranking out of the stereo system. Some folks were dancing. A lot more were busy pounding beers. In the center of the living room, a small crowd had gathered around Lance and Darcy. There they were, our hero and his chosen lady, our king and queen, our shining stars. Darcy clung to Lance as if he were the brass ring on a carousel. Yeah, that too. Add that to the list after shining star. I watched her stretch up and whisper something in his ear. You didn't have to be a rocket scientist to guess what she was saying. I could almost hear her breathy, sexy murmur:

"I just got so excited thinkin' 'bout next year and Florida State and the future . . . baby, I think I need to be your wide receiver . . ."

I couldn't help checking Darcy out. Her shimmery blue halter dress didn't leave much to the imagination. It hugged her body and stopped mid-thigh. Not that her long, sinewy, sunkissed legs, or slender, shapely body could have been much better in my imagination than they were in real life.

I glanced at Jules. She had on a pair of silvery gray velvet pants that sat low on her hips, a sleek, steel colored T-shirt and platform sandals. Hip. Alluring. But not flashing much flesh. More smart and cool than sexy. I looked back at Darcy's Spice Girls getup. "How come you never dress like that?" I asked Jules.

She didn't miss a beat. "Costs a lotta money to look that cheap."

"Darcy's pretty sharp. She pulls all As," I said.

Julie raised an eyebrow. "That's not all she pulls."

"I'm just saying she's not stupid."

As Julie and I stood observing her, she kissed Lance's neck. Then she teased his ear with her tongue. An open invitation.

Lance looked at her and raised an eyebrow. "Really baby? Here?" his expression said.

Darcy took his hand and led him through the sea of admirers to continue what they'd started without the audience, in someplace private.

Julie and I checked out the bar and the munchies, stopped to talk to some pals, and danced a couple of songs. Then we headed back out to the porch. It was a warm, humid night, the moon hazy behind a thin film of clouds. We cooled down with a couple of beers we drew from the keg into blue plastic cups. A little home movie action was in progress out here, Billy Bob having traded the sweet-faced girl for a video camera. He had the camera trained on Tweeder and some hair-challenged guy who was way past high school and busting out of a faded blue-on-blue football jacket.

Tweeder was interviewing the guy and holding a whiffle-ball bat, although from what I could tell, the bat had nothing to do with the video. "You graduated in nineteen-eighty and you still come to the football parties?" Tweetie asked.

"Never miss one," the guy said proudly.

"That's the spirit," Tweeter encouraged. "Okay! Well, you ready to be on America's Hilarious Home Videos?"

The bald guy was down with the plan. "Yeah. Absolutely."

"Okay. Pick up this potted plant and hold it with both hands above yer head."

The bald man snapped to the order. You could tell he was psyched to be one of the guys.

Tweeder turned to Billy Bob. "You gettin' this?"

"I got it."

Tweeder oh-so-casually but oh-so-firmly

whacked the bald guy in the nuts with the whiffle-ball bat. I flinched. The bald guy collapsed on the ground in pain.

"Jesus," Julie said softly. I had to agree it was kinda harsh.

Billy Bob finished filming, and pulled the camera out of the guy's contorted face. He and Tweeder took slugs off their beers. "That was funny," Billy Bob guffawed.

"Yeah, that was funny," Tweeder echoed. "That's what I'm sayin'. They should change the name of the show to America's Funniest Shots in the Nuts."

Jules and I took that as a signal to look elsewhere for some party fun. We saw some folks we knew out on the lawn and we wandered over. "Yeah, and how 'bout when Lance got off that perfect spiral even though that moose was in the process of flattening him . . ." We wandered away.

Inside, it was more of the same. " . . .when he faked left and then . . ." We didn't stick around for that conversation, either.

Eventually, we went crawling back to Billy Bob, who'd given up the video camera and had installed himself at the kitchen table and declared himself unbeatable at "quarters." Of course, he was so far gone that the table was littered with quarters that hadn't made it into the glass. And each time he lost, he had to chug, which only led to more quarters that hadn't met their goal.

Julie took a seat across from him and dug in her bag for a quarter. "Alright, fancy boy," she addressed him. "You ready to show me your dinner?"

A dozen or so people had gathered around to watch the game, including Tweeder, still holding the whiffle-ball bat. Billy Bob looked nervously nauseous as Jules tilted her pretty face up slightly and positioned the quarter on the bridge of her nose. She released the coin, gently lowered her head, and the quarter rolled smoothly down her fine, straight nose, bounced once on the table—a nice, high bounce—and *swish!* into the glass of beer it went.

"Nothin' but the net," she said with satisfaction. Yup, Jules was good at winning, too. It ran in her family. She just didn't believe the hype, was all.

I applauded. So did the other spectators. Julie gave a modest bow—a nod of her head, really. Then she fixed Billy Bob with a stare. "Chug," she said.

It always seemed like the wrong tactic to me to make drinking the price for losing. Especially where Billy Bob was concerned. He was happy to chug whether he won or lost. But I could see him struggling to get the Bud down right now. He gagged. He was filled to the brim already. Marinated.

"Thinkin' about callin' some dinosaurs?" I asked him.

"Figured I'd—" He let out a really nasty, rumbling belch. "Figured I'd give 'em a holler," he said. And he was up and out of his seat before he'd even finished his sentence, running blindly for the proverbial airline bag.

"Billy Bob's gonna puke!" Tweeder yelled excitedly.

Billy Bob went for the first door he came to. He threw it open, giving everyone in the kitchen a clear view of Lance and Darcy, going at each other on top of a bucking, bouncing washing machine in operation. Darcy's shiny blue dress was pushed up around her waist. Lance's jeans were around his ankles.

Billy Bob didn't give them a second look. He charged through the door into the little laundry room.

"What the fuck—!" exclaimed Lance, grabbing at his pants and yanking at Darcy's skirt and glaring at Billy Bob all in the same second.

Bill Bob staggered over to the dryer, side-by-side with the washing machine. He opened the dryer lid right next to Lance and Darcy, stuck his head inside, and let loose.

People were whooping and yelling from the kitchen. Lance and Darcy had gotten to their feet and were covering up, mortified. Billy Bob finally emerged from the dryer, wiped his mouth with the back of his hand, and grinned at the lovebirds interruptus. "If yer hungry, I left a few hotdogs here in the dryer." He turned toward his audience in the kitchen and pumped his fist in the air. "Oh, yeah! Puke 'n' rally! I'm back!"

Jesus, I thought. Maybe this was our cue to leave.

As far as places to get with your girlfriend, I'd definitely vote the cove underneath the railroad bridge over a laundry room. The inlet that wound from the gulf and opened into the cove carried a gentle sea breeze. Most of the cloud cover had broken up, and a few of the brightest stars pierced the inky sky. The moon was about half full, and the silvery light streamed in through the open windows of my car and bathed Julie's face.

I leaned over and kissed her, simultaneously turning the knob on the side of her seat and putting it down as far as it would go. She wound her arms around me and pulled me on top of her. She kissed me back with fiery intensity, her mouth exploring my mouth, her tongue probing. I covered her body with mine, aware of her lean but strong torso, her hands caressing my back, her hips pressing against mine, the heat of our bodies.

I felt myself come to attention. Julie's body was tense with desire. We ground against each other, kissing each other's faces as we struggled out of our clothing. I helped her pull her T-shirt over her head and shrugged out of my football jacket. She grabbed my belt buckle. I was more than ready. She unfastened my pants and I pushed them down around my ankles with one hand, reaching inside her bra with the other. God, her skin was so soft. I teased her nipple with my fingertips and felt it harden. She kissed the curve of my neck. I buried my face in her sweet, silky mane of brown hair.

It would have taken too much time to get totally naked. We were greedy for each other, impatient. All the pent-up energy I hadn't gotten out sitting on the bench today was channeled into our bodies. We groped and stroked and kissed, wet and hot with need. When I couldn't stand it a second longer, I entered her, strong but gentle. Julie gave a sweet moan. I made the first slow, potent thrusts. Oh my god, life was good. My breath came faster and shorter. We pumped harder. Faster. I could feel myself going over the edge . . .

Just as we climaxed, I heard a train speeding

toward the bridge. Our sounds of pleasure joined the powerful noise of the train cars passing overhead. We clung to each other as the chug-chugging grew fainter and disappeared into the distance. I caught my breath and opened my eyes. Julie was looking at me, her eyes shining, her brow glistening with sweat.

"I love you, Johnnie."

I smiled at her. "I love you, too."

"Isn't this better than football?" she whispered.

"This is better than anything."

"Do you really mean that?" she asked.

"Yeah, I do," I said. And it was true. When we were together—I mean really together, as in two bodies as one—time slipped away, lost its hold, dissolved. There was nothing but the moment. Nothing but Julie and me. Nothing but desire and pure sensation. Nothing but wanting—and getting. That and the fact that in this game, at least, I was a fully active participant . . .

"You believe there's something greater than Coyote football in West Canaan?" Julie teased softly. "That's sacrilege. What would your father say?" She grabbed my football jacket and wrapped it around herself. Then she kissed me again.

I kissed her back. Right at that second, I really didn't give a damn what my father thought.

Later, we left the car down by the cove, and walked up to where the train tracks led over the bridge. We stood a few feet away from the rails, looking out over West Canaan. You could see the streetlights and the lights of the houses, like fallen stars, in neat suburban rows. The Canaan mall dominated the landscape. Across from it was the familiar H-shaped building of West Canaan High. The football stadium was behind it, its lights dark, as if it were taking a well-deserved rest after the big win. I figured at least a few of my team were sprawled out down there on the field, drunk on booze and victory, reliving the game play-by-play, and talking trash about all the girls they weren't with, right now. I felt lucky to be up here with Jules.

But maybe she wasn't as satisfied. "There are kids in Brazil who are famous for train surfing," she said, seemingly out of nowhere.

Where had that come from? I turned toward her. "You going to Brazil?"

"No, but I'd love for us to surf a train right outta West Canaan." Well, at least the problem was our location, and not me.

"You're drunk," I stated.

"Define drunk."

"What?"

Julie started laughing. "Mox, you and I have

been shot down behind enemy lines. We woke up in the Twilight Zone. West Canaan, Texas. Fuckin' and Football, that's all there is."

"What are you talking about?" I asked her. But of course she was right. Drunk, but right.

She was on a roll. "Thank God I like fuckin'," she said.

I laughed. It worked for me, too. But before I could even get a word in to agree, Julie was off and running again. She could get like that when she'd been hitting the brewskis. "I love you, Johnnie. Have you heard from colleges? I really wanna see the East Coast, Boston, New York . . . the Atlantic Ocean."

"Am I in this conversation?" I asked. It was hard to keep up.

"I'm sorry, Johnnie. I'm just fired up." Julie blew out a breath.

"About what?"

"You, New York and . . . Pedro." Suddenly, she reached for my crotch, and got me in hand.

"Whoa!" I said. "Pedro, would you like to say a few words?" I made my voice all nasal and sing-song. "Yes, I would like to thank señor Mox for tonight's opportunity to perform—"

"C'mere, Johnnie." Julie giggled. "You make me laugh," she said sweetly. "I love the way you are when we're alone." She kissed me. I kissed her. We kissed some more.

4

The sun had barely broken the horizon, but on the field, we were hot and sweaty. Practice had begun in the gray, grim light of pre-dawn. Lap after lap around the field. Up and down the bleacher steps. Push-ups—hands, fingertips, more, faster. Kilmer loved yanking us out of bed and making us hurt before we were fully awake.

Dad and Joe Harbor, and a bunch of West Canaan's most loyal, stood on the sidelines sipping coffee out of paper cups. Chet McNurty was there, too. Chet had played ball with Dad and Joe Harbor back when they were Kilmer's Coyotes. His son, Tad, was a sophomore receiver.

The Dads all hupped to attention as the coach

blew his whistle. All those years down the line, and it was still an automatic reaction. On the field, Lance took the snap, executing a flawless bootleg rollout before firing a perfect spiral. The guy was a star, sure enough. From the sidelines, I watched the ball sail through the crisp air and connect with the receiver, a new kid named Johnson, who sprinted across the field to snatch the pigskin.

"Attaboy, Lance!" the coach shouted, ignoring Johnson completely. "First string offense, take water. Okay, Dummy-Os, follow your Dummy-O Q.B. into the mud for a scrimmage." That meant me. Dummy-O. As in Dummy Offense. As in, you poor slobs who aren't worth the shit you're sliding on. "C'mon, Mox! Pick It up!" Kilmer badgered. "Your attitude is earning you laps right now."

I broke into a grudging jog and led the second string onto the field. I wasn't all that eager for any extra laps this morning. I clenched my teeth—or rather, bit down hard on my mouth guard. Damn, I used to love this game. In theory I still did. But how into something could you get when it earned you the label Dummy-O?

And there were Dad and the other Dads, still thinking Kilmer's farts didn't smell. No doubt the coach had hammered their asses thirty-something years ago the exact same way he was hammering ours now. And they talked about it as if it was the time of their lives.

Well, damned if I was gonna worship the guy like that. I decided to have a little fun. Rattle Kilmer's cage. Shake things up a little. Huddled in our second-class circle, I outlined the play. I broke the huddle and clapped sharply.

We all hustled into formation. I could feel the looks from the spectators and the rest of the squad. *Just what kind of weird formation does he think he's pulling?* But I glanced around and Dummy-O had it right. No running backs. Four wide receivers stacked in pairs on the left. A fifth receiver on the right.

"What the hell kinda offense is that?" I heard Tweeder's voice call out.

I looked off to the sidelines. I met Lance's stare. He was grimacing. I think he was genuinely embarrassed for his ol' pal Mox, here. I shot him a cartoonish grin and started counting. "Thirty-four, sixty-two, fire drill seventy-nine, hut, hut—"

SCREEEE! The shrill, metallic screech of Kilmer's whistle cut the air. "What in Jesus's name you doin', Moxon?" he blared. "What kinda lu-lu formation you pullin'?"

I hesitated. *Thou shalt not worship false gods*, I told myself. "It's a secret," I finally said. A nervous giggle punctuated my sentence.

"Your Dummy-Os can't even run a draw and

you got secret formations?" Coach Kilmer was livid. I hadn't expected anything less. "Shit-for-brains! This ain't no fuckin' sandlot!"

"It's the Oop-de-Oop," I defended myself. "Mississippi Valley State's averagin' sixty-six points a game with this offense."

Behind the coach, Lance was waving his arms wildly, signaling me to shut the hell up. I appreciated how my friend was looking out for me, but quite frankly, I was enjoying myself.

"Oop-de-Oop?" Kilmer asked softly, the calm before the storm.

I nodded. "Go with all wide receivers. Overload the strong side, burn the defense one-on-one on the other—"

I saw Kilmer lunge at me. I caught my breath sharply, and took a step back. He charged, grabbed my facemask and shook my head like an ape shaking a coconut. I struggled to stay on my feet. I reeled with dizziness and a wave of nausea.

"You got a bad attitude and you don't listen!" he screamed into my face. "We do things here *my* way! You think you're goin' to some fancy school? Bullshit!" I could feel every eye in the stadium on us. "You've shown me the kinda smarts that makes me wonder if you know the difference between a sneeze and a wet fart. You're gonna be a second stringer all your life, boy!" He let go of my mask. "Now go on!"

I lifted my helmet off, and spit my mouth-guard into my palm. I hated the bastard.

A burst of laughter floated across the field. I turned toward it. Over on the side, some of the fathers were having a yuck-yuck at my expense. It was a game. Kilmer's game. Bag on Sam Moxon's boy. I could see my father tighten with anger. He said something to the other Dads. I'll venture a guess as to what. "I stood up to it. So will he," he might have been saying. Then he turned away to sulk.

Well *I*, Jonathan Moxon, was not going to let coach Kilmer get to *me* that way.

In full gear, we ran in place. That was after our post-scrimmage laps. On Kilmer's signal, we dropped to our toes and fingertips and gave him thirty. On our feet again. Down for another thirty. Again. Again. Again. Assistant Coach Bates circulated through our ranks, making sure no one was sloughing off.

I was toast. Burning, aching muscles. Not even enough left in me to hate Kilmer right at this moment. Or fear him. Fun? Sport? You tell me.

"Chop your feet!" the coach commanded us. We lifted our legs high as we ran in place. "Chop 'em! Dive!" Down we went. "Back up! Chop those feet! Dive!"

I don't know how, but I managed to keep the

pace. Lance and Wendell chopped and dove, too. But Billy Bob, struggling next to me, was sucking air, trying to get his wind. I could hear him gasping and wheezing. He could barely pry his feet from the muddy ground. He made a feeble attempt at a push-up and collapsed on his big belly, face in the mud. He let out a wounded animal sound.

Whoa, what was up with the B-meister? That blow to the head he'd taken at the victory line the other night hadn't been any love tap. For all we knew, the guy had a full-blown concussion, and nobody had even bothered to find out.

"Billy Bob!" Kilmer shouted at him. "Get up, you pansy ass!" Billy Bob didn't move. "I said get up! You gonna let some puppy-nosed freshman beat you outta your position?" he threatened.

Billy Bob managed to lift his head. "No, sir!" he responded.

The guys took up the chant. "Billy Bob! Billy Bob!"

Billy Bob pushed himself to sitting. He looked up at the coach like a little boy. "I'm dizzy, Coach. Lemme catch my wind."

Kilmer wasn't buying. But I bet you aren't surprised. I wasn't. "That what you say to the other team's nose guard as he's runnin' past your pansy ass on the way to kill Lance?" the coach roared. Then he shifted gears and made his voice all high and girly. "I'm dizzy, Mr. Nose Guard. Could you wait, please, while I rest a spell?"

Laughter from the troops. Some of them.

Coach Kilmer knelt down beside Billy Bob and whacked him with his clipboard. On the head. Like Billy Bob's head hadn't taken enough of a beating. "You're my sergeant on the field, Billy Bob. You gotta show these guys what dedication is! Move it! Move it!"

Billy Bob rallied. The old "show the guys" routine. But it worked. "Yes, sir!" Billy Bob said, making a pathetic attempt to stand.

I couldn't bear it. I offered Billy Bob my hand and pulled him up out of the mud.

"Mox, thanks," he said. "I ain't feelin' right."

Coach Kilmer whirled on me. "Back off, Mox! The Nancy boy stands on his own or he don't wear my Varsity Blues!"

I backed off. I despised the son-of-a-bitch, but I'd pushed him as far as I could afford to today.

Miss Davis's class. I stretched my legs out and settled back in my chair. Billy Bob sat across the aisle, doodling aimlessly. The margins of his notebook were filled with crudely drawn footballs. Billy Bob had been making the same doodle since about third grade.

In one corner of the room was a life-sized, scientifically correct plastic skeleton. Anatomy charts covered one wall, the male body and the female, a front view and a back of both, buck naked and copiously labeled with all the proper names for all their intimate and not so intimate parts. On the facing wall there were anti-drug and anti-smoking posters. A "Mothers Against Drunk Driving" button was stabbed into the bulletin board between the newspaper and magazine clippings.

They called it "Health" class, but we all knew it was what was commonly known as "Sex-Ed." In other words, the class where they tried to talk us out of doing what our bodies were talking us into doing. In the battle of Miss Davis vs. raging hormones, it was no contest every time. At least from where I was sitting. But it was kind of fun to watch pretty, ditzy Miss Davis go on about the sweatier side of life.

Davis was busy writing something on the board. Without giving it too much importance, I watched her butt go up and down gently as she wrote. She tended toward the efficient secretary look—crisp suits and jackets and moderate pumps. But if you looked hard—and sometimes I did when the lesson was boring—she had a good shape and an attractive face, under her not entirely unappealing rectangular glasses.

She turned back from the board, and we could see that she'd written "SEXUAL REPRO-DUCTION," in big block letters. I snuck a look at Billy Bob, and he grinned. It was going to be a good class today.

A case of twitters broke out around the class-room. Some spontaneous applause. Miss Davis looked flustered. "Yes, well . . ." she said. "I feel it necessary to move beyond the giggles sur-rounding the common nomenclature associated with sexual reproduction."

Billy Bob's hand shot up.

Miss Davis looked at him. "Nomenclature is a collection of terms or vocabulary specific to a subject," she said, not bothering to wait for him to pose the question.

Billy Bob put his hand down. You could see Miss Davis take a long breath as she mentally warmed up for the Big Topic. "Alright, now," she began, taking the plunge. "I want everyone to say, 'penis penis penis, vagina vagina vagina.' "

Total silence in the classroom. Miss Davis had surprised us with an unusual play. Her very own Oop-de-Oop.

"Say it!" she repeated with more force.

We said it. Softly. Tentatively. With much embarrassment. "Penis penis penis, vagina vagina vagina." I myself was blushing. I mean, a word's a word, but some words are more private than others. And hey—there were girls in the room, too.

But Miss Davis was nodding, proud of our progress. "Good. Great. Before we go further, I feel we need to mention and throw away common street sayings for different sex issues, and we need to be clear on what we want to consider appropriate language for us to use during this unit. Today, we are going to be talking about the male erection."

Everyone looked straight ahead. Even though I know that my instinct, for one, was to cop a glance at my crotch.

Billy Bob's hand shot up, again. Miss Davis looked at him. "Hand down, Billy Bob!" She sounded flustered. You could tell she had her whole speech planned out, and she wanted to get it done and over with. "So . . . what are the few slang expressions for the male erection that we want to identify and discard?"

No one volunteered anything. Saying "penis penis penis" out loud, the whole group, as if we were sitting around singing campfire songs, had been enough.

Miss Davis shifted uncomfortably. "Alright, then. I'll start you out with two of the four I think are most common, and see if you can get the other two." She swallowed hard. "Okay . . . Hard-on and woody, okay?"

Snickers. Giggles that people tried to suppress. Where was the lady going with this?

She waited for someone to come up with the other two. So to speak. But no one was game. "C'mon!" she said, frustrated. "Anyone think they know the other two?" She paused and you could see her trying to regain her composure. "Or even one of them?"

Elliot Mertz raised his hand timidly. Elliot was a major geek. But Miss Davis was grateful to him. "Elliot. Yes, Elliot."

"Umh, ah, boner? Is boner one of them?"

I struggled not to laugh. Was Miss Davis going to ask for a volunteer to demonstrate next?

"Yes!" she said jubilantly. "Yes, boner. Very good. Boner is good. Anyone else?"

Billy Bob raised his hand. Oh, my god. What was he going to come out with?

Miss Davis apparently didn't want to gamble on that. She looked away. He called out. "May I go to the bathroom?"

She looked relieved. "Yes, go," she said, clearly eager to get rid of him. Billy Bob stumbled out of his seat. He still looked pale from this morning's workout. Meanwhile, Miss Davis wasn't letting go of this erection thing. Okay, I don't mean that literally. I'm just telling it like it happened.

"Anyone else know any others before we move on," she prodded.

More silence. Even though you knew that every guy in here was going through an impressive list in his head. Suddenly it seemed absurd that we couldn't just come out and say it. I raised my hand. If she wanted it, why not let her have it. So to speak. Not literally. You know what I'm saying.

"Mr. Moxon. Share with us," Miss Davis encouraged me.

"The male erection?" I began. "Pitching a tent, sporting wood, the icicle has formed, the march is on."

"Thank you, Jonathan," Miss Davis said primly. I wondered if this would bag me that A in Health.

But I wasn't finished. "Stiff, stiffy, Mr. Mortis, rigor mortis has set in, the Saint is marching in, chubbed, chubby, atten-hut, ten-gun salute, the banana is ripe." My classmates broke into applause. At this very moment I was a star. Out of the corner of my eye, I caught Elliot taking frantic notes. "Jack's magic beanstalk, tall Tommy, the flesh rocket, mushroom on a stick, Mr. Mushroom Head, Johnnie get yer gun—" a personal favorite— "the brick in my jeans, 'Gee your nuts smell terrific' and . . . Pedro."

"Pedro?" Miss Davis asked, her eyes wide with awe.

At that second, Billy Bob burst back into the

room. I noticed his face and shirt front were sopping wet, like he'd been trying to wake himself up by splashing water on himself. He wove toward his desk as if he'd been downing sixers behind the mini-mart.

"Billy Bob?" Miss Davis said.

His answer was to keel over. He hit his desk on the way down. A collective gasp went up from the class. Billy Bob's eyes were closed. His face was as gray as the linoleum tile floor. He was out cold.

Billy Bob lay on the green canvas camping cot in the nurse's office. I held his head up with one hand, and with the other, I offered him sips of cool water from a Dixie cup. He was starting to look a little better. The nurse was on her lunch break, and she'd left me playing candy striper, giving me instructions to make sure Billy Bob rested quietly.

The office door opened, and none other than the one and only Coach Bud Kilmer entered. He looked at Billy Bob. Then at me. Then back at Billy Bob. "How you feelin', son?" he asked with a show of concern.

Suddenly, Billy Bob was looking pale again. Scared. "Can't hold down any chow, sir."

Kilmer nodded. "Must be nerves. Don't worry, son. You're playin' every minute of the upcoming game." Every minute? The nurse had told Billy Bob not to move. Let alone play football. And this was supposed to reassure Billy Bob?

"Sir," Billy Bob said weakly, "she thinks I shouldn't play, 'cause of when my head got whacked last week."

Kilmer frowned. "She doesn't have a district title to win. *You* tell *me*. Are you alright to go?" he demanded.

No, he's not alright, I wanted to say. Look at him. He's losing his lunch. Fainting in class. His brain's wobbling around inside his head. Play him and it might just leak out his ears.

But Billy Bob just nodded gingerly. "Yes, sir," he said.

The coach smiled and patted Billy Bob on the hand. "That's my boy," he said. He strode to the door and then he was gone. He didn't shower me with a single word.

5

The irresistible smell of char-broiled T-bones wafted through the air. Joe Harbor, star quarterback's star dad—and our host—tended to the thick slabs of meat laid out on his shiny, new Happy Cooker, like offerings to the god of backyard barbecues. The late afternoon sun was still hot. The grown-ups stood around admiring the oversized grill, the perfect cuts of meat, Joe's searing technique . . .

The coals flamed up suddenly, spewing red, orange and blue tentacles. Lance's dad thought on his feet. As the rest of the parents jumped back, Joe Harbor drew a water pistol he just happened to have in his apron pocket and fired into the flames. They sizzled. The beef sizzled. It was all good.

Lance's stepmom, holding an extra-large, clear plastic cup full of some slushy blue blender drink, held forth with my mom and a couple of the other moms. "Bull fuckin' shit!" she proclaimed noisily. "That's what I told my sister, I did. I said *bull fuckin' shit*. You don't want to marry him. Not because he's your first cousin, but because he lost a testicle in the Gulf, and he's already got four kids." Clearly, Colette Harbor had had a few of those blue things. "Family. Fuck 'em, y'know?" she said.

My mom nodded politely.

Lance, Jules and I wandered over to the edge of the shimmery turquoise-bottomed swimming pool. Billy Bob was on our minds.

"I agree with Coach," Lance was saying. "I need Billy Bob to protect me."

"When he's a hundred percent, he's the best in the game. I'm just nervous after that shot he took the other night."

"They're letting him play?" Julie asked, incredulously. "He's got a serious injury."

"It's only his head," Lance protested.

"Would you play with a concussion?" Julie asked disgustedly.

Lance shrugged.

After the feast, we sat around at a picnic table piled high with corn cobs and beer cans. Most of the parents had been pounding those blue things, or slugging back the beers. We'd sneaked a couple for us, but basically, I was fully satisfied with the juicy steaks and the fresh corn.

Joe Harbor reached across the table and mussed his youngest son's hair. Troy looked more like Lance than like Julie. And he wanted to be a football star like Lance, too. What Texas boy didn't? "Yep, gonna hold our Troy back a year," Joe Harbor said, "so he'll be bigger for frosh try-outs. Eighth grade ain't so bad, is it, son?"

Oh, man, the guy was sick. Excuse me for thinking badly of my girlfriend's father, but he was gonna keep Troy back in school so he'd be big enough to squash all the other kids into the ground?

But Troy smiled. He seemed to think it was a great idea.

"Our Kyle's so excited," my dad chimed in, not to be outdone. "He had that ankle problem, but he's ready to go now. Ain't that right, son?" He swiveled around, as if it were the first time it had crossed his mind to look for my brother. "Kyle?"

Kyle was sitting under a leafy pecan tree in the lotus position, his legs folded underneath him like a pretzel, wearing a white Zen prayer robe. His eyes were locked in a meditative trance, as he stared at the barbecue grill and the glow of the dying embers.

"He's very spiritual," my mother said.

"C'mon," Colette Harbor said harshly. Her lips and tongue and teeth were blue—West Canaan blue—from those frozen drinks she'd been guzzling by the bucket. "He's a freak." Well, takes one to know one, but I guess I'd have to admit that my brother is a little weird. My mother looked stung.

Joe Harbor shot his wife a look, and reached down to nab a football that was lying near the picnic table. "Shame nobody had the mind to hold us back when we were kids, eh, Sammy-boy?" he asked my father. "Aw, hell. I didn't fare so bad." He stood up, dropped back a number of steps, pumped the ball and lofted it to Lance. Lance didn't get up from the table. He just picked the football out of the air.

"Toss me one, son," his father said. "Let's show 'em yer ol' pop's still got it. Button hook left. On three."

Lance looked at me, shrugged, looked back at his father, and stood up. Joe Harbor took a three-point stance, and then darted across the backyard. I'll admit it. He was pretty fleet-footed for an old dude whose belly flopped up and down as he ran. Lance fired off a perfect spiral. Of course. His Dad sucked it in. A smattering of applause from the steak-stuffed fans.

Joe Harbor came back to the table, took a little bow, and then shoveled the ball to my father. "C'mon, Sammy-boy. Let's see it, ol' man."

Dad grabbed the pigskin eagerly, ready for the challenge. He turned to me. "Let's show 'em how it's done."

Was there no escape from football—ever? "Dad, you're gonna fall in the barbecue," I said feebly as Dad backed toward the grill, holding the football aloft.

"Slant left, on three," Dad commanded. "And don't talk back to your father." He tossed me the ball. I caught it as he took his stance. He cut and waved clumsily for the ball. Without getting up, I half-heartedly let it fly. It overshot the mark—that mark being Dad, stumbling backwards and trying as if his life depended on it to get his hands on that ball. He managed to graze the pigskin, but it wobbled out of his hands and plopped onto the grass.

"Guess bad hands run in the family," Lance's father guffawed. I could feel Jules cringe next to me.

"And what's that supposed to mean?" my father asked, tightly.

"Can't take a needlin', eh, Sammy-boy?"

"If Kilmer weren't such a prick, my boy would be startin' quarterback," my father spat out.

Stone-cold silence at the picnic table. My father had dared to suggest that Lance Harbor was replaceable. In West Canaan, that bordered on sacrilege. Finally, Lance's father started to laugh. Chet McNurty joined in. All the parents were focused on my dad and Mr. Harbor.

"That so?" Joe Harbor confronted my dad. "Think he's first string?"

"That's right," my father said. I winced. Couldn't we go back to the Happy Cooker and the blue drinks and the harmless picnic fun?

"I smell a challenge," said Chet McNurty.

Joe Harbor wheeled on me. "How about you, Johnnie?" he demanded. "Think you're better than my boy?"

The kids were all focused on us now, too. "Dad," Julie protested, "how can you ask him that?" Well, at least one person here was looking out for my best interests.

"Simple 'nuff question," Joe Harbor said, not even bothering to glance at his daughter. "Well, Johnnie?"

I was hot with embarrassment. Everyone waited for my answer. Of course, I was supposed to step up to the challenge. Step into my big football ego. But was I better than Lance? I hadn't seen any action on the field all season. How did I even know, anymore? I certainly didn't care as much as Lance, and maybe that automatically meant that I wasn't good enough. At that moment, I was more than ready to do some train surfing to Brazil. Jules looked set to accompany me.

"Tongue stuck, boy?" her father goaded me. "I think it's best we settle this matter once 'n' for all." He picked up a beer can. For one absurd second, I thought we were going to settle this by trying to out-chug each other. Then Joe Harbor put the beer can on his head. "Remember William Tell? Get going, Lance. Let's show them Moxons what it takes to start fer Kilmer's Coyotes."

"Stop it, Dad," Julie said. "This isn't funny." She was right about that. It was deadly serious. Lions in the prideland, the alpha male challenged for his right to rule.

Colette Harbor took a drunken, blue-mouthed step toward Julie. "I'm your mother and I demand that you . . . listen!"

Julie flashed Colette a disgusted look that said it all. Mother? Never. She didn't waste another look on her father. She just stormed away across the backyard, and headed into the house.

"Kids!" Colette Harbor said with annoyance.

But Joe Harbor frowned at her. "This here's

'tween the men," he told her. As far as he was concerned, she was as far out of the picture as Julie.

Help came from an unexpected corner. "Lighten up, Dad," Lance said. Okay, Lance may be West Canaan's Big Cheese, but there's a reason he's my friend. He knew the Dads were getting out of hand. "I don't wanna—"

"Do as you're told, boy!" his father cut him off. "I mean it. Knock off this here can. Show 'em what you're made of."

"C'mon, Lance," cheered his little brother. "Nail the can! Nail it!"

Lance looked at me and raised his shoulders. It was easier just to give in. His father positioned himself solidly, the beer can balanced on his thinning hair. Lance put about ten yards between himself and his dad, and pulled back the ball. Joe Harbor stood confidently. Lance threw. The ball hit the can squarely, and sent it flying off his dad's head.

"Now *that's* a startin' quarterback," Joe Harbor said.

Lance looked pleased with himself, a little drunk on Texas football.

My father didn't waste a second grabbing a beer can and assuming the same stance as Joe Harbor had taken. Troy Harbor shagged the football from the lawn and brought it to me, the dutiful puppy bringing in the morning paper.

"Dad, c'mon, this is dumb," I objected. A grown man balancing a can of beer on his head. And why? So he could prove his son was better than his friend's son? A bit of regressive behavior there, if you know what I mean.

"Looks like the boy's 'fraid to lose," Joe Harbor harassed us. "Lot different on the bench, now ain't it, Johnnie?"

I looked toward Lance for support. His face was blank. Well, I guess he figured he'd taken his turn, why shouldn't I? I looked toward my mom. She stared back, as in, meet the challenge, Johnnie. No support from anyone. Well, what did I expect? This was West Canaan. Where was Jules when I needed her?

Fuck it. What choice did I have? I stood and took aim at Dad. I let 'er rip—an angry, dead on throw. Bull's-eye! The dregs of unconsumed beer splattered my father as the can flew into the air. Dad puffed up with pride.

Joe Harbor grinned back. "Lookie there. Now we're havin' fun." He turned to Lance. "Let's paste 'em, boy." He picked up one of the cans from the lawn, and stepped back five yards farther than he'd gone before. He balanced the can.

This time, Lance didn't hesitate. He fired. A perfect strike. Nothing less from Lance.

Joe Harbor nodded at my father, all business. "You're up, Sammy-boy."

Troy shagged the ball again, and shoved it into my arms. Wasn't this over yet? This was pathetic. I threw the ball down, repulsed.

"Oooh," went Joe Harbor, like an eight-year-old. "We're sportin' some 'tude now."

"Pick it up!" my father screamed at me. He stepped back five yards farther than Joe Harbor had. "Show 'em you're a winner! Pick it up!"

"You can do it, Johnnie," Mom chimed in.

"Aaaugh, sit on the bench," Joe Harbor provoked me. "Show us what ya do best."

"Be a winner!" Dad again. "Pick up the damn ball!"

"He's a chicken," Troy Harbor squeaked. "Bawk, bawk, bawk . . ." Everyone was yelling at me at once.

"I raised ya to be a winner!" my father hollered. "So win, boy! Dammit! Fire that fuckin' pigskin!"

I grabbed the thing, fury pumping through me. I pulled my arm back, took aim, and hurled the damned all-important ball. The football smashed square into my father's face. I felt a split second of satisfaction. Then chagrin, as Dad went down. Jesus, what had I done? Blood poured from his nose. He glared at me from the ground.

* * *

Fourth to last game of the season. You *know* I was counting down. Coyotes vs. the Greenville Hornets. Somewhere up there in the bleachers was my dad, sporting an impressive splint and bandage contraption on the middle of his face. Joe Harbor had already made a bunch of jokes about it. "How many campers that pup tent accommodate?" he'd asked my dad before the game.

Did I feel guilty? Fuck it. Football is a dangerous game. Except, of course, if you stayed on the bench. Which is where I sat, watching as the Hornets pushed the ball past mid-field to the Coyote 42. Not where you wanted the opposition to be. Their quarterback dropped back and threw a screen pass. We forced their receiver out of bounds just shy of a first down.

The clock stopped. A minute 49 remained in the game. Fourth and inches, and we were behind 17–21. We were in trouble.

And Billy Bob was in even worse trouble. He stumbled off the field and went straight for the oxygen tank, sucking down the O₂ like a man dying of thirst. Lance strode over to him, looking worried. I mean, you shouldn't get the idea that Lance Harbor was above worrying about his fellow man.

"Shit," I heard Lance say. "Another first down

73

and they'll be in field goal range." Fellow man? Scratch that. It was all about the victory. Or lack of one.

I went over to them and patted Billy Bob's back. Lance and I exchanged an uncomfortable look. "Hang in there," Lance encouraged Billy Bob. Okay, so maybe it was part fellow man, part victory. This was war. And Lance was Heap Big Warrior.

On the field, the Hornet fullback was stopped up the middle for no gain. Finally, a little luck for our side! The Coyote fans were on their feet and cheering. "Our ball! We got the bastards!"

Without thinking about it, I'd gotten to my feet and was cheering, too. Maybe our fate was changing.

Coach Kilmer strutted proudly on the sidelines, as he sent his offense out to turn around the game. His men jogged onto the field with renewed spring in their step. All except Billy Bob, who was tethered to the oxygen tank like an umbilical cord.

"Get in there, Billy Bob! I need you for one more series!" Kilmer yelled.

Billy Bob rose slowly, with obvious effort. I could see him drawing this fish-out-of-water gasp. He held his head as if it might spin off at any moment. He was pathetic as he wobbled toward the field.

I felt a wave of pity for the B-meister. I hustled over to him to help him get where he was going. "You okay, big guy?" I asked him. "Billy Bob?" He just had to rally for another minute of playing time.

Billy Bob didn't respond. The guy was a zombie. I put my hands on his shoulders and stopped him from going into battle.

"Moxon! Get yer ass back on that bench!" commanded the coach.

I turned toward him. We exchanged the coldest of stares. At that very moment, I was sure that Kilmer had sold every shred of humanity and empathy to the devil in order to win all those trophies.

While we assaulted each other with our eyes, Billy Bob wandered out to the offensive huddle.

The West Canaan fans roared their excitement. They could taste victory. You could just feel it. The Coyotes broke huddle and lined up. Lance called the count.

Billy Bob looked bad, swaying like a blade of overgrown grass. Lance took the snap. I saw Billy Bob collapse. No one had even knocked him down. He'd simply passed out, as far as I could tell. Fainted all on his own, a repeat of health class. But unlike in health class, there was an immediate stampede over the body. The Hornet defender charged past, untouched.

I bet Lance never even saw the guy who blindsided him. But I did, and he was huge. Lance was crushed on the turf. I grimaced in sympathy. The football rolled free. The Hornet defender scrambled off of Lance to try to recover it, but Wendell was on it, grabbing it away.

As Wendell got the ball, I saw that Lance was clutching his knee. He writhed around on the Astroturf, crazy with pain. He thrashed. No way was he getting up.

With a jolt of apprehension, I was on my feet and racing over. Lance lay moaning on the ground. Joe Harbor was sprinting down from the bleachers, Jules and Colette trailing behind him.

Meanwhile, Billy Bob had come to and gotten himself up. He wove toward Lance, calling his name.

I know how Billy Bob felt. I mean, yeah, Lance is number one and I'm a far distant second—and it's not the easiest place in the world to be. But it's all part of the game. I admire Lance. He's the real deal. A star. And I love him almost like a brother. I couldn't stand to see him so badly hurt.

"Please . . ." Billy Bob moaned, and I could hear tears in the guy's voice. "Please be okay. Please, Lance!" But Lance wasn't okay.

Five minutes later, the stretcher arrived. It was bedlam on the field. The medics had to push through the worried fans to get to Lance. Joe and Colette Harbor were stunned. I had my arm around Jules—she was tight with worry. We stared as they moved Lance onto the stretcher. The cheerleaders had gathered around us, and Darcy was crying. I bit my lower lip.

And then, before I'd even had a chance to think about what Lance's injury meant to *me*, Assistant Coach Bates was gently separating me from Jules and handing me the football.

The fans were broken-hearted. I don't think I'm exaggerating if I tell you that big men were weeping big tears, hyperactive kids were paralyzed with grief, and various folks were doing violent things to the stuffed Coyote dolls they toted to games for good luck. I knew they thought the season was over. That I wasn't worth the Charmin I wiped my butt with.

But they hadn't seen me in action. I threw the football with Coach Bates, warming up my arm. I was worried about Lance. Of course I was. But I was also nervous and excited that the ball was mine.

The medics carried Lance off the field, an entourage following the stretcher. I paused, ball in hand, to give an empathetic little wave to Julie. Coach Kilmer was with the stretcher, too. He stopped, turned and stared at me. I paused, ball in hand, and stared back. For the next 1:09 minutes of play, we were in this together. Weird.

Kilmer saw Lance into the ambulance. Then he jogged back across the stadium floor. Back to business. Our offense was ready to take the field. I felt a rush of adrenaline. The coach came over to me. "Watch me for the signals," he said. "Stay focused. Don't worry, son, I'm behind you." He gave me a pat on the helmet, but we both knew there was no fondness in it. Fuck Kilmer. I was gonna do this for *me*. For West Canaan. I escaped to the field.

I could feel everybody holding their collective breath. I glanced up at my family in the bleachers. Dad and Mom were just about down on their knees praying at this point. And Kyle? Well, he'd been praying—about who knows what—for the past few months. I figured I could use their prayers.

I entered the huddle. The guys were filthy and tired. Morale was at a low. I could see it in their eyes. I felt like Mr. Clean in my pristine uniform. I glanced at Billy Bob. His eyes glistened with tears.

"He's hurt bad, Mox. It's my fault."

There'd be time for this later. Right now I

needed to concentrate on getting the job done. "Uh, Side Post eighty-eight on um . . . two." I clapped. We broke huddle.

Coach Kilmer paced nervously. But I was pumped. With nerves. With challenge. This wasn't anyone's backyard barbecue.

I stood ready behind our center. I yelled hut and took the snap. I dropped back. The blitz was on. I felt a surge of strength. I ducked one rusher, a huge, meaty guy. A Mack truck. I rolled out of the pocket and set. No hesitation. I threw deep.

Tweeder streaked downfield. He had a step on the defender. Good boy, Tweetie. I watched my throw arc perfectly into Tweeder's hands. I felt a rush of accomplishment. The Hornet tackler just managed to bring Tweeder down in bounds.

West Canaan went nuts. Literally. They threw peanuts. And soft drinks. They danced like ravers. They shared hugs. "That's my boy!" I thought I heard my father holler. "My boy! *My* boy!"

I grinned. Every cell in me grinned. I remembered why I love this game. But we hadn't won. Yet.

The clock was still ticking precious seconds. Forty-nine, forty-eight, forty-seven. I yelled for my teammates to line up. The Hornets were deliberately slow, running down the clock. Which kept ticking. Thirty-five, thirty-four, thirty-three.

The Hornet mascot, one big, stupid killer bee, dragged a black-clad leg to indicate that they could hold on to the game if they just managed to take their time.

I felt a shot of anger. I immediately called for the snap, and drilled the pass out-of-bounds—directly at the big Hornet's face. Nailed him. And stopped the clock. Absolutely a more worthy smack in the nose than I'd given my dad, I must say.

"Right between his fuckin' eyes!" I heard a fan shout out. I laughed. The clock showed twenty-nine seconds left.

The blue-on-blue clad crowd was on their feet. "Touchdown! Touchdown! Touchdown!" they chanted.

I looked at Kilmer. He signaled a play, gesturing precisely, commanding with his hands. No room for misinterpretation. Man, that tired routine? We'd done it a thousand times. Well, I hadn't. But the team had. And the team before us. And before them. When was Kilmer gonna retire some of those old saws?

I considered what to do. We huddled. I called a different play.

The roar of the crowd was so loud that I took

a step back from the huddle and raised my hand to quiet them. No use. We broke huddle. My men set up on the line of scrimmage.

Out of the corner of my eye, I could see the coach making large, angry gestures to get my attention. I didn't so much as glance his way. I stepped up behind the center. I screamed the count. Snap! I dropped back, rolled left, and handed off to Wendell.

As soon as I put the ball in Wendell's hands, I started downfield, while Wendell backtracked. It was a trick play. Now *he* was passing to *me*. I sprinted past the Hornet defenders. At the five yard line, I turned, and the ball was right there for me. Wendell had gotten off a beautiful pass.

But I got hit from behind, by a monster from the other team. I felt myself spin. I went down on one hand, pushed myself up, and dove for the end zone.

Touchdown!! Yes-s-s-ss!! I was in! I'd made it! My god, was it sweet.

The gun went off. Hornets 21, Coyotes 23.

It was a riot in the stadium. All of West Canaan was pushing onto the field. Sheriff Bigelow, in a big white cowboy hat, was coming at me, his gun drawn. Wait a minute. His gun drawn? I was relieved as he raised his arm and fired into the air, a victory salute. I caught sight of my father and mother, holding hands as they ran toward me. I flashed them a triumphant thumbs up.

And then I was being lifted high into the air by my teammates, high onto their shoulders. I looked down on the throng of cheering people—cheering for us, cheering for me. It was a nice view. And this once it was mine.

6

I hate hospital waiting rooms. I was here when my cousin Brandon totaled his car, and for a while there we didn't know if he was going to make it. I was here again when Lance and Julie's mother was sick. Jules and I weren't going out yet, but Lance had been my best buddy forever, and we all knew his mother was dying. There had been a lot of tears that night. There were always tears in a hospital waiting room.

Now I sat close to Julie on the hard, vinyl covered sofa, and I could feel her tension. Lance's knee had been shattered, and he was in surgery as we waited. I knew what Julie was thinking. *For what? To get a lopsided excuse for a ball into the end zone?*

Joe Harbor looked grim. Troy was fighting tears—a pint-sized tough guy in training—and Darcy was giving in to them, her make-up streaking down her cheeks. Colette Harbor, liquor on her breath, was pacing around the waiting room like a caged cat. "Fuck, I haven't been here since my miscarriage," she muttered. She was really good for morale.

And how could I leave out Coach Bud Kilmer, Sir? He stood in the middle of the waiting room, his presence taking up more space than a normal person.

A man and woman maybe ten, twelve years older than I was entered the waiting room, a brand-new baby snuggled in the woman's arms. Snuggled in the man's arms was a clean, new football, tied around its fattest part with a blue ribbon. They approached the coach.

"Coach Kilmer?" the new father said. "Excuse us, but the nurses said you were here. Is Lance alright?"

"Still in surgery," the coach answered gruffly. Then he glanced at the baby and brightened. "This new li'l gridder yours? Congrats, and you too, Mary Bether." He bent toward the baby and gently unwrapped the yellow blanket it was swaddled in cocoon-style. He touched the baby's tiny, fat toes, gave its leg a light squeeze.

Kilmer, a baby-lover? I couldn't get my mind

around it. But no, he was just checking out his newest Coyote-to-be. "Look at them strong legs. He'll be a mean ol' linebacker. Just like his pa."

The new dad couldn't have looked prouder.

But the baby and its linebacker legs were forgotten as a white-smocked doctor pushed through the waiting-room doors. He came straight toward Joe Harbor. "Your boy is out of surgery, Mr. Harbor. Should be able to visit—"

"How long's he out?" Lance's father cut him off. And he wasn't talking about the anesthesia.

I strained for the answer. We all did. "Any chance for this season?" Coach Kilmer demanded.

The doctor turned toward the coach. "Lance tore every ligament he could. Going to need more surgeries over the next few months just to repair them all."

"How long!?" thundered Joe Harbor.

"Minimum year and a half," the doctor said. I felt my chest tighten. That was almost halfway through Lance's college career. And then the doctor dropped the real bomb. "If ever . . ." he added.

There were a few moments of mute shock. Lance Harbor, star, was finished. In one brutal moment of game time his future was over. Joe Harbor let out a low moan. I looked at him.

Actual tears were welling up in his eyes. Julie went to his side and took his arm.

While everyone was focused on the doctor and Joe Harbor, I sneaked through the doors that led to Surgery. I knew where the recovery room was, and I made a beeline for it. A number of the guys from the team had been in here at one point or another. But that didn't prepare me for the extent of the machinery holding Lance's plaster-encased leg up in the air, or all the tubes running into him, or his ghost-pale face, eyes closed, mop of sandy blond hair against the stark white pillow.

I approached his bedside. "You're gonna be fine, Lance," I whispered.

His eyes fluttered and he struggled to open them. He was still fighting off the anesthesia. But he looked at me just for a second, and flashed me a grateful smile before he passed out, again. I patted his arm, careful not to touch the IV. "Just take it easy," I said. I went out to rejoin the others in the waiting room.

Our whole group was now gathered around the doctor. "I don't understand what you're saying," I heard Julie tell him.

"I'm just saying that I'm amazed Lance wasn't having problems before this. I removed a helluva lot of scar tissue from that knee."

We all looked at Coach Kilmer. His expression didn't give away a thing. "Never said anything to me," he told Joe Harbor. I thought about that needle I'd seen the trainer sticking into Lance's knee. And the way the coach had slammed the door in my face. Right, Coach. You didn't know a thing. Not much.

Kilmer must have felt me drilling into him with my glare. He turned toward me and glared back. It was a mean look. And at that second, he still had the power to scare me. I didn't say anything. This was not the time or place. It wasn't going to do anything for Lance.

The couple with the new baby, off to one side while the doctor spoke, edged toward Coach Kilmer. He paid no attention to them. He gave me his back, and took a new tone with Lance's father. "Lance is a gamer," he said, as if he were giving a team member an inspirational lecture. "That's the kinda competitor your son is. Played with the pain. So damn proud I could cry."

Like that self-serving bastard had a single tear in his rock-hard heart. Joe Harbor didn't look like he was buying. Jules was glowering at him, too. She had his number, for real. Darcy looked as if she didn't know what to think, and Colette Harbor looked—well, drunk. But the new parents were clearly in awe of Coach Kilmer, Sir. They exchanged looks, nodded, and the man pushed a pen and the football in the coach's direction. "Excuse us, Coach," he said insistently. "We gotta go, and we'd sure be honored if you'd sign this football. Hospital sends one home with every baby boy."

I think Coach Kilmer welcomed the distraction. He bestowed a smile on the happy family. "Of course," he said, taking the football and pen. "Can't start teachin' the three R's too early."

"Rushin', receivin', 'n' punt returns," the new father recited.

The coach signed the football and handed it back. I wanted to pummel him. And he knew it. He looked at me, again. "Mox, get on home," he said, feigning a fatherly attitude. "Get some shut-eye. The Harbors appreciate you being here, but there's nothing more you can do tonight."

Right. I'd won the game for him. Now he wanted me out of his lying, conniving face. Julie came up next to me and put her hand on my arm. "You go on," she said gently. "I'll stay with them."

I looked into her eyes. I could see how worried she was, but she gave me a little smile. The only sane voice in the pack. The only one who seemed to care about the people more than the players.

"Sure?" I asked.

She nodded.

I gave her hand a squeeze and turned to go.

"Well, I guess I should be leavin' too," Darcy said. "This being a family thing." Darcy had been pretty quiet the whole time. I think she wanted an excuse to book. And who could blame her? It wasn't a party in here.

Darcy was, in fact, looking for the party. And there was one. Despite Lance's bad fortune. There was always a party after the game. Win or lose. You celebrated or you drowned your sorrows. It was the Way around here.

She sat beside me in the passenger seat of the Moxmobile, wiping her streaked make-up off with something she'd dug out of her big, blue gym bag. She re-applied it like a pro, her hand steady even though we were driving through the streets of West Canaan. She still wore her cheering outfit.

"Thanks for the ride, Mox," she said, as she finished freshening her lipstick. She put the make-up back into her bag, and pulled out something red and slinky-looking. I did a double-take, almost veering into the other lane. She pulled a pair of high-heeled sandals out, too. Then she began to take off her cheering sweater.

"What the hell're you doing?" I yelled.

Darcy pulled the sweater over her head, revealing her lacy, black bra. She tossed the sweater into the gym bag. "Changin'," she said, matter-of-factly.

It was all I could do not to drive into a tree. Darcy Sears in a sexy bra is kinda hard to avoid staring at. She was full in all the right places—two that I had to fight not to look at, at that moment—slender and toned in all the other ones. "Oh, c'mon," she said, a teasing note in her voice. "I'm wearing underwear. Covers up the same as a bathing suit. If this really bothers you, I'll wait."

"Whatever," I said. "I can handle it." *Eyes on the road*, I told myself. *Eyes on the road*. I repeated it in my head like a mantra, as she scrunched out of her skirt and down to her matching, black lace panties. It wasn't that I was trying to look. I stared at the road, but I could see her—just about all of her—in my peripheral vision.

"This has been the worst night of my life," Darcy sighed, stuffing her cheering clothes into her bag.

I couldn't really concentrate on what she was saying.

"You really aren't looking, are you? You're sweet," she said, with a little laugh.

"Lance is gonna be okay," I assured her, distractedly. I kinda felt like I needed to bring his name into this conversation.

"His career's probably over," Darcy said flatly.

I hadn't been thinking football at that very second. "But you guys are gonna be okay," I said. "I mean, you love each other."

She swiveled toward me, still down to her bra and panties. "Things change, Mox. I don't wanna think about it right now."

"Sorry," I said. *Eyes on the road.*

"S'okay. I mean, what about you and Jules? Is there a future?" Was that a question—or an invitation? It was pretty clear I could take it however I wanted to.

And I'm not gonna come on all ethical and moral and pretend I wasn't tempted to pull over in a hurry and jump her. Darcy was a sexy, beautiful girl. But she was Lance's sexy, beautiful girl. And Lance was in the hospital with his leg in some kind of complicated, architect-designed contraption right now. And Julie was with him.

"Yeah, well . . . I'm graduating. Jules has another year," I heard myself say. Hello. Who was that talking? Sounded like someone who didn't quite want to say he wasn't available. "I mean, I love spending time with her," I said feebly.

"Things change," Darcy repeated, pulling her dress on over her bra. "You're the starting quarterback now."

We'd reached the party. I didn't know

whether I was relieved or disappointed. Music blasted out of the house. A bunch of people littered the lawn, drinking out of blue plastic cups. "Okay, you're here," I told Darcy.

"You're not comin' in?" she asked. She looked right at me as she pulled her shoes on.

I felt the temptation passing. Sort of. "Not tonight," I said. "Doesn't seem right with Lance all fucked up."

Darcy dropped her gaze and busied herself straightening her dress. She opened the door, grabbed her gym bag, and let herself out. I watched her walk around the front of the car. Sexy and beautiful. She came all the way around, and leaned into my window. "You don't always have to do the right thing, Mox." She whispered, as if she and I already had a secret. "We'll continue this anytime you want."

I let out a long breath as she went up the front walk. I noticed Tweeder going wild on the lawn. Drinking two drinks at once. Laughing like a hyena. Generally getting rowdy. Darcy disappeared into the house as a State Trooper car pulled up behind me. A uniformed officer stuck his head out of the car window and addressed the kids on the lawn.

"How we all doin' t'night?" he called in Tweeder's direction.

"We all doin' fine!" Tweeder called back, imitating the trooper's slightly nasal twang. "Partyin'!" he added.

A bunch of folks out on the lawn with him laughed.

"Great, great, congratulations," the cop said.

"Congratulations to you, too," Tweeder said, still mocking him.

The trooper got out of the patrol car. His partner got out, too, the motor idling. "Congratulations for what?" asked the first one. He was starting to sound annoyed.

Tweeder took a slug out of his cup. "For gettin' to wear such cute mount-me hats?" I couldn't help laughing. Tweeder was sheer drunken nerve.

The trooper fell for it. "Mount me?" he asked.

"Don't you think we should make out first?" Tweeder howled.

Everyone cracked up. Myself included. Except the troopers. The one guy's face contorted in fury. His partner raced around the car and put a restraining hand on him. "Okay," said the second officer, "alright, we just wanna make sure that nobody drinks and drives."

Tweetie went right up to them. Handed them his drinks. No lyin' here. He really did. "In that case, will you hold these?" he yelled.

The cops took the drinks from him. Before anyone knew what was happening, Tweeder had taken a running leap into the patrol car and was peeling off down the block. The two police-men were left holding the blue plastic cups, and staring in shock as their patrol car screeched around the corner and out of view.

All the kids on the lawn broke into hoots and hollers. Just another post-game party. Laughing, I took off, too.

The mini-mart was basically deserted. Just me and the old dude at the register. Everyone else was out post-game partying. Or recovering after the game. Or not recovering—leg up in some hospital bed. I felt sorry for Lance as I dis-tractedly put my bottle of root beer on the counter with a bag of tortilla chips. I waited for the clerk to ring me up.

Instead, he came around from behind the reg-ister, took my root beer, and headed to the bev-erage cooler. He put the bottle back, pulled out a six of ice cold beer, and put that on the counter in front of me.

I looked at him. He was smiling broadly. Huh? Oh, yeah. I was the quarterback. I looked back down at the cold brewskis. Okay. I could get used to this.

"Great," I thanked him. "How much?" I reached into my football jacket for my wallet.

The clerk put out his hand to stop me. "Your money's no good here."

Whoa. A six-pack without an ID—and I kept my money, too. Good deal. I arched an eyebrow at him. Was he sure?

He nodded and gave me the thumbs up. Well, if he insisted. He put my beers and chips into a brown bag and I carried them out. Maybe Darcy was right. Things changed.

I didn't have anywhere special to go. On the one hand, I guess it would have been fun to share my big win with some folks, soak up the limelight, let my ego get a little exercise. On the other hand, I'd meant what I'd said to Darcy. It didn't seem right to be partying hearty when Lance was all smashed up. Besides, on the real, I kind of wanted to have a little private time to savor my success. It would be too weird to just step into Lance's life because I'd played a few minutes of good ball. Okay, excellent ball.

I left my car parked in the mini-mart lot, and I headed down Main Street, no particular destination in mind. I sort of liked walking through town when everything was closed up and dark. It was quiet. Peaceful. I cracked open one of the beers and sipped it. I had fastened my belt through the plastic six-pack rings, so that the rest of the beers dangled by my hip. They thudded against my leg as I walked, but I didn't mind.

I crossed the street at Main and Willow. At least I started to. Suddenly, a patrol car, lights flashing, came flying out of nowhere and nearly killed me. I jumped back, spilling some of the beer on my hand. I heard a squeal of metal and rubber, as the cruiser fishtailed into a 180, doing a dramatic about-face and coming to a halt about twenty yards from me. I was the only one on the street. What did they want? I hid the remaining brewskis behind my back. My heart pounded.

"Jonathan Moxon!" A familiar voice boomed out of the car's P.A. system. "You're under arrest for not being naked with some sophomore chick who wants to bathe you with her tongue. Uhh . . . remove your clothes and get in the car."

Jesus. Tweeder. He still had possession of the cruiser. I squinted into the bright headlights.

"We're all naked in here, Mox, and there's handcuffs and shit to play with!" he announced.

I went over and peered into the cruiser. Tweetie was in there with three girls. Three naked girls. He hadn't been lying. The girl sitting closest to him grabbed the police mike. "Mox!" her high voice boomed across Main Street. "Tweeder threw my clothes out the window. Will you come keep me warm?"

I figured that making it with three girls at once in a stolen police car was probably a felony in Texas. But knowing Tweeder, he thought it was worth a few hundred years in the slammer. I shrugged out of my jacket. "I can't go with you," I told the girl, "but I'll give you my jacket." I handed it through the window to her.

The other girls pounced on it immediately. Wolves fighting over a hunk of meat. In that minute nine I'd played, my jacket had gone from being worth a couple of Andrew Jacksons, to being an incredibly hot and valuable item.

From farther up Main Street, I heard the wail of a siren. More flashing lights came zooming into view. And this time, the guys in the patrol car were the real deal. "Sorry, Mox," Tweeder said quickly, "gotta bail. Ladies, hold on to yer nipples!" The naked girls all put their hands on their breasts as Tweeder floored the gas pedal and fled, leaving a stink of burnt tire rubber.

The freebie brewskis were starting to do their thing. As my legs got a little loose, and my mind relaxed, I found myself wishing I could be with Jules. Maybe not the most logical thing to want to share my victory with the one person in all of West Canaan who wasn't infected by football. And with Lance in the hospital I knew she wouldn't be up for any partying. But maybe I'd just go over and see if she was awake and say hi.

I stowed the three remaining brewskis in my car, and left it parked. Julie's house wasn't very far. The lights were out, but I crossed the lawn and rapped softly on her window anyway. I waited. Knocked again, a little more firmly.

A couple of seconds later, the window opened. Julie poked her head out. "Hey," she said. I could hear the radio playing softly.

"Your weren't sleepin'?"

"No. I was lying in bed naming my unborn children," Julie said, gently mocking me. I guess she *had* been sleeping. But I was glad I'd gotten her up. I felt better just seeing her face. The day had been long and full of trick plays.

"How's Lance?" I asked.

Julie shrugged. "Out of anesthesia. But he's gonna have to do it all over again in a few weeks."

"I'm gonna go back and see him tomorrow," I said.

Julie nodded. There was a beat of silence. Somewhere in the distance, a cat let out a wail. "Heard you played a great game," Julie finally said. We hadn't talked about it in the hospital. It had hardly been the time or the place.

"You missed my big moment," I said, half making fun of myself, but also kinda wishing I didn't feel so weird about claiming my place in the limelight. For once.

"I guess I had a good excuse," Julie said.

"Right." I thought about her speeding off in the ambulance as I charged onto the field and took Lance's place. "The whole thing's strange."

"Strange to be a god now?" Julie's words took on an edge. In her bedroom, Jewel was singing her hit song, "Foolish Games."

"I don't know," I said. "I mean, we did win, y'know? It feels weird. I've been walking around for a while . . ." It was hard to explain. It had been such a roller coaster of different feelings.

"What's wrong, Johnnie?" Jules asked, her voice softening. "You want me to get dressed and come out there?"

I was suddenly very tired. Physically. Emotionally. It had been some ride today. "Nah, I'm gonna go home," I said. "I just wanted to see you. It's been a really weird night . . . whatever. Hey, turn it up. I like this song."

Julie arched an eyebrow. "You always call this 'vagina' rock."

"It *is* 'vagina' rock," I said. "I like vagina rock." Call me a wuss for admitting it, but these sweet, lyrical songs could really get under your skin. Especially if you were feeling pretty emotional already.

Julie went and turned up the music. I sang

along, doing my best to imitate Jewel's high, clear voice. *"These foolish games . . ."* I sang. I took a few steps backwards, and whirled around on the Harbors's front lawn.

Julie's mellow, bright laughter floated out the window and caressed me.

7

It was all over town. How Tweeder had stolen a State Trooper's patrol car, and how he and some of the other guys on the team had exposed themselves to the Ladies' Auxiliary. Pulled out their wangers, and pressed them against the glass of the Alano Club while the ladies were rehearsing the Christmas pageant.

Tweeder's older brother, Wilson, had been in Murray's Bar the next day, and he'd heard everyone talking about it. Now, over burgers and fries at the Coyote Cafe, he told Tweetie and me how Sheriff Bigelow was complaining to Chet McNurty. "So the sheriff tells McNurty the players are runnin' around lawless, hopped up on beer and painkillers. Those 'xact words," Wilson said, popping a fry into his mouth.

"Party on!" Tweeder exclaimed, waving his burger around excitedly.

"McNurty didn't think so," Wilson said. "Told Sheriff Bigelow that what you did wasn't right."

"Chet McNurty?" I asked. "Man, my dad and Joe Harbor are always tellin' stories about how outta control that guy used to get post-game in the old days. And Tad McNurty's not exactly the quiet type, either."

Wilson shrugged. "I dunno about that, but Chet and the sheriff were ridin' high and mighty, I'll tell you that much. Talking how they couldn't let you guys get away with that stuff anymore. Of course, Coach Kilmer was sittin' right nearby and they knew it. It was just a matter of time before he checked them. Went right over to Sheriff Bigelow and asked him if his boys were giving the sheriff too much trouble. Bigelow backed off right away."

"Let's hear it for the coach," Tweeder said, holding up his Coke in a toast.

"The coach is an asshole," I put in.

"Yup. But he's *our* asshole," Tweeder said. "What happened next?" he asked his brother.

"Well, Murray came over with a pitcher and he got in on it," Wilson said. "Asked the coach if he thought we'd beat Elwood and Gilroy."

"Shit, yeah," Tweeder exclaimed.

"We only have to win two of the next three to lock up the District Championship," I put in.

"That's what Kilmer said." Wilson nodded.

I felt a flicker of annoyance. It was one thing for me to be all reasonable and rational about it. But what Kilmer was basically saying was that he wasn't betting on us winning all three games. Not with Lance out. Not with me in. "Nice vote of confidence," I said sarcastically.

Wilson looked uncomfortable. "The sheriff thought you looked good on Friday. Said so to Kilmer."

"And what'd the S.O.B. say to that?" I asked.

"Whoa, Mox! Down, boy! Okay, maybe he's bumming over the fact that Lance has enough silver in his right knee to stir all the coffee in the county."

"We're all bumming about that," I said. "It sucks big-time. Now what did Kilmer say about *me*?"

Wilson took a big bite of his burger. Took his time chewing and swallowing. "Tell me!" I said harshly.

Wilson shrugged. "Fine. He said, 'They all get themselves a sweet hand now 'n' again. But Moxon sure ain't got what Lance had.' Okay?"

"Our asshole," Tweeder said, nodding.

"Then Chet McNurty said he supposed it was too far into the season to get ourselves a new Q.B.," Wilson recounted. "The way they got Wendell from that other school district. You asked for it, Mox. You man enough to hear it?"

I felt the burn. I was humiliated. And furious. I'd been a star out there on Friday. What the hell made them think I wouldn't be a star again? "What did Kilmer say about that?" I demanded.

"He didn't. Joe Harbor showed up right then, looking like Godzilla on a mission."

"Godzilla rocks!" Tweeder said.

His brother rolled his eyes at him. "Tweeder. you're a moron, you know?"

"Yeah, but I'm *your* moron. So what did Lance's ol' man do?" Tweeder wanted to know.

"Well, he was pissed," Wilson said. "He charges right up to Kilmer like he's gonna tackle the guy, and he starts screaming about how Kilmer's ruined his life, ruined Lance's career. The sheriff jumps in and tells Joe to take it easy. Says Lance and the Coyotes're damn fortunate to be blessed with a fine coach like Bud Kilmer!"

"To a fine asshole," Tweeder chimed, holding up his near-empty Coke glass.

"Shut up, Tweetie," I said. This was important. I waited for Wilson to go on.

"Well, Lance's dad tells Kilmer that Lance

said he shot up his knee with painkillers. That Kilmer knew Lance was hurt. Said Kilmer pushed him when he shouldn't have. That he'd trusted Kilmer and now their chance for Lance was gone. He was yelling his head off in that bar. Crying almost, I swear. Told the coach he better fix things. Wanted to know how he was gonna make it all up."

Good luck, I thought. So Kilmer was now a fallen idol at the Harbors's. It only took Joe Harbor thirty-something years to catch on. But better late than never. I felt vaguely sorry for the guy.

"So then . . ." Tweeder prompted.

"Well, that was the wildest part," Wilson said. "First the sheriff and Murray get their hands on Joe Harbor and try to walk him out of the bar. The coach plays all nice and stuff and tells them to let him go. Goes right up to him with this look like, 'I feel your pain.' Says, 'Joe, I know this has been rough on you. I'm sorry about that. Look, I'm headin' out. I'll talk with you outside. I've got some news will make you feel better.' "

"Insincere son-of-a-bitch," I said.

"Yeah, but he's *our* insin—". I whacked Tweeder and he shut up.

"Truer words have never been spoken," Wilson said. "Joe Harbor goes and waits outside for Kilmer. Meanwhile, Kilmer's in the bar telling everyone, 'We take care of our own around here, don't we?' And he's patting people on the back and shaking hands with every damn person in there, and they love the guy. He shakes my hand and I can see he barely remembers I was on his squad a few years back. Second stringer," Wilson said, looking right at me.

"Yeah. Well," I muttered.

"Anyway, a few minutes later I leave the bar, and Kilmer's in the lot behind the strip, his face in Joe Harbor's face, giving him some serious shit. I got up as close as I could behind Kilmer. Heard it all. 'Don't you ever come out of pocket with me again,' he says to Harbor. 'You do and I *will* ruin your fuckin' life. Let's see how the kid heals. I know the coach of the junior college in El Paso. You keep your fuckin' mouth shut and I'll get 'im a walk on over there next year. Best I can do, alright? Don't ever come at me like that again.' Harbor looked sort of scared. Gave this feeble nod and got into his truck and drove away," Wilson finished.

El Paso Junior College? Suddenly the anger went out of me and I just felt sorry for Lance. El Paso's team was like an overgrown J.V. Lance, who'd been rockin' a stadium of thousands, Lance who'd been bound for glory . . .

The next game was away. Waynesboro, population 32,469, as the sign says. Home of the

E.J. Camp

Billy Bob

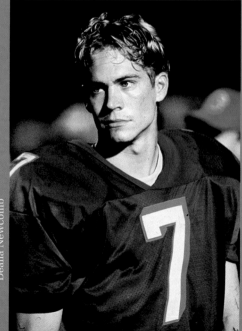

Deana Newcomb

Deana Newcomb

Broncos. One of our long-time enemies. Billy Bob did his usual as we rolled into town on the team bus. "And yea though I walk through the valley of the shadow of death I fear no faggots from Waynesboro," he intoned.

I was in the back of the bus, going over plays in my head. Coach Kilmer kept sending me these covertly threatening looks, reminding me I better do exactly what he said. But at that moment, I didn't care what a bastard the guy was. In fact, it just made me even more determined to show him—to show everyone—that the last game hadn't been a stroke of pure luck on my part.

I'd been sick nervous the night before, but I wasn't gonna show it now. I was the starting quarterback. I was strong. I was invincible. Hear me roar. Whatever. Behind us were caravans of Coyote supporters. In fact, there was a sign at the West Canaan town limits that said, GOOD LUCK, COYOTES. LAST ONE OUT OF TOWN TURN OUT THE LIGHTS. I wasn't going to disappoint our fans.

I couldn't get the ball off. I scrambled from the pass rush, but two massive Broncos were on my ass. Tweeder was open, and waiting for my pass. But it wasn't gonna happen. I had to think quick. No. I had to act. I ducked under one of the brutes' truck of an arm and decided to run with the ball. I dodged the other. Yes! I put on a burst of speed and saw daylight. I wove. I sprinted. I danced. Alright, I could do this! I ran as hard as I could. As hard as I ever had. A white-shirted Bronco came out of nowhere. I ran harder. I could feel him a hair's-breadth behind me. I hugged the football and burst into the end zone.

TOUCHDOWN! Yes-s-ss! Oh, my god, I'd run the damn ball right into the zone for a T.D.! I threw the ball on the ground and raised my fists over my head. Touchdown!! The West Canaan section in the bleachers was on their feet. Jumping, shouting. Soft drinks spraying into the air. I was immediately mauled by my teammates. Billy Bob grabbed me and picked me up easily, showing me off to my adoring fans. I was laughing with pride and happiness and the sheer feat of what I'd pulled off.

It was Coyotes 66. Broncos 3. Fourth quarter. Twenty-nine seconds left in the game. We were victorious! I was victorious! Coach Kilmer stood on the sidelines, his face showing nothing. I was victorious! Take that, Coach Bud Kilmer, Sir!

"Gimme a M!" I heard Darcy call out from the line of cheerleaders. "Gimme a O! Gimme a X!" From up on Billy Bob's shoulders, I looked over and had a good view of her swinging her dark blue and light blue pom-poms crazily. "What's that spell?"

"Mox!" the rest of the cheering squad joined in. "Go, Mox, go!"

I grinned. It didn't feel so shabby to have a dozen gorgeous girls in skimpy outfits yelling your name.

The Bronco fans were as miserable as we were happy. Their coach stood in desperation on the sidelines as people in the stands booed and jeered. The boos got louder when he didn't even bother to send his team back on the field.

The gun sounded. Coach Kilmer started across the field to shake the hand of the Bronco coach. Suddenly, another gun blast from a different direction. I felt a jolt of fear. But it immediately dissolved as I thought about Sheriff Bigelow, firing into the air at our last game. I looked around for him.

Instead, I saw a tubby, middle-aged man in a Bronco red jacket rushing his team's coach with a drawn pistol. "Sixty-six to three? Seven straight defeats! You bastard! This is all your doin'!" he screamed maniacally. Coyotes and Broncos alike bolted over and wrestled the guy to the ground almost immediately. Billy Bob put me down on the ground, and we rushed over. One of the Broncos pried the gun out of the man's hand. "Lemme go!" he kept screaming while pinned to the turf. "Gotta *kill* this losin' bastard!"

The Bronco coach stood frozen, stunned. Coach Kilmer sprinted over to him. "Tom! Tom! You okay?" It was one of those rare moments when he was actually, genuinely concerned.

The Bronco coach nodded slowly. He unzipped his jacket and began unbuttoning the shirt underneath. I stared at him. What was he doing? He pulled open his shirt to show Coach Kilmer a neon orange bulletproof vest underneath his clothes. "Been gettin' calls," he told Kilmer solemnly. "The wife made me wear this Kevlar vest."

Believe it or not. It can happen. This is football, and this is Texas.

MOX IS A FOX, read the banner that some anonymous someone had left on my windshield. Yeah? Hey, check it. The girls think I'm kinda cute, I thought. I guess I was amused. I guess I was flattered.

But I had to hold back a little grin as Julie pulled the banner off my windshield and threw it on the ground. She'd been waiting for me in the school parking lot when the team bus had pulled in. I was glad to see her, even if she had missed another one of my "big moments." But she was genuinely happy for me that I'd cooked ass today. She even listened tolerantly to me as I called the most critical moments of the game like a radio announcer.

A shiny, new Mustang convertible pulled up alongside us. Bright red. Miss Davis was in it. Miss Davis? In a red Mustang convertible? Whatever. She waved at me. "Great game, Jonathan. I'll see you in class."

I felt a puff of pride. It was kind of fun being the star. "Nice car," I observed to Julie as Miss Davis drove off. "On a teacher's salary. She's single, too."

But Jules was in her own space. "I'm gonna go with my dad to see Lance," she said.

I felt instantly guilty. While I was lapping up the hero stuff, Lance was in bed with his leg up in traction. I'd seen him the other day, surrounded by flowers that weren't nearly as fresh or alive as they'd been the day he'd gone down on the field. Once famous, now forgotten.

I just about forgot him, too, as I saw the Pud—the voice of station WPHD—coming at me with his microphone. I'd seen him interview guys before. Lance. Wendell. Never me. He nearly bowled Jules over as he squeezed in between us. "This is Olin Buchanan of WPHD," he said into his mike. "The Pud, and I'm here with Jonathan

Moxon, the Mox, fresh rising star quarterback of the West Canaan Coyotes." The guy had this oily smooth voice and he talked a mile a minute. "Mox, how does it feel to be out of Lance Harbor's shadow and showin' everyone you've been underrated? And we all wanna know 'bout you plannin' to play ball in the Ivy League . . ."

He finally took a breath, and I was able to get a word in edgewise. Although I guess I have to admit that all his praise and smooth words felt kind of good. "Gee, Lance Harbor left really big shoes to fill," I said, in what I hoped was a modest, properly honorable way. Maybe Lance was tuned in on his hospital radio. "I don't know if I'll ever get the job done like Lance did. Heck, the Ivy League? I don't know. I thank God and my teammates for the win today. I'm just one man, y'know? I'm one man."

The Pud looked pleased with my little speech. I could almost hear the sound bite now: *I'm just one man, y'know? I'm one man.* Not bad.

He thanked me, withdrew his mike, and was gone as fast as he'd come. I looked at Julie and smiled. She just rolled her eyes. " 'Gee'? 'Heck'? You even thanked God. *You* are a scary superstar."

I was disappointed. "Oh, c'mon, Jules."

112

"You referred to yourself as 'one man.' You're really enjoying this."

"Why not? It's a trip." I couldn't help the way the smile sneaked back on my face. I'd played great ball today. And everyone knew it. Was it so terrible to let myself enjoy that?

8

All of a sudden, I was all over town. Or at least pictures of me were. I couldn't stop Dad from putting up a huge sign on our front lawn that said HOME OF QUARTERBACK JOHN MOXON. It was corny, but it made Dad happy. Meanwhile, Mom had bought up a few hundred copies of the West Canaan *Register*—the one with the picture of me taking up most of the front page, and a headline that screamed "Moxon's Arm Breaks Broncos!"

Wilson Tweeder had told me that they'd taken down Lance's picture at Murray's Bar, and replaced it with one of me. And sure enough, there was that sound bite. *I'm one man.* Picked up by the local television news, and played over and over. I even heard it blasting out of the sound system at the supermarket.

But don't think I was livin' the easy life. On the field, I still had to prove myself. Still had to show the guys I could lead the team the way Lance did. Kilmer didn't believe it for a second. Made it perfectly clear.

A few days after the game in Waynesboro, he was on the sidelines, staring, evil-tempered, at a crisp crack-of-daybreak practice. Some of the dads had been talking about him and Joe Harbor, and he probably knew it. My father was drinking coffee in the bleachers with Chet McNurty, and every once in a while, the coach would glance over at them, paranoid-like.

On the field, Wendell took a hand-off up the middle. He gained four yards.

We went into a huddle. "Let's razzle-dazzle them Dummy-Ds," I said. I didn't mind the dummy bit quite so much now that it was the other guys. "Package six. Pitch left reverse, Q.B. swing left."

Wendell shook his head. "That play never works. Something always screws up."

"We'll have some fun. C'mon," I said. I just wanted to try something a little different than the usual routine. Wendell shrugged. We clapped. Broke huddle.

Billy Bob lagged behind and got close enough

to whisper to me. "This ain't the one where I trot downfield and pretend I'm lost?"

I sighed. That blow to the head hadn't made the B-meister any sharper, that was for sure. I called time out. Everybody returned to the huddle. "Billy Bob," I told him, "This play's for you. The formation makes you eligible."

"Eligible for what?" he asked. Jesus. How many years had Billy Bob been playing this game?

"The ball. I'm gonna throw you the ball, Billy Bob."

"But I ain't no eligible receiver," Billy Bob wailed.

"See what I mean, Mox?" Wendell said.

I looked at Billy Bob. "Just catch the damn ball," I answered.

We broke huddle and lined up nose-to-nose with the Dummy-Ds. Billy Bob set as a tight end on the far right. At least he'd gotten that much right. I took the snap, pitched out to Wendell, and led him around the left side. Johnson swept across the backfield and took the hand-off from Wendell for a reverse. So far, so good. Wendell was wrong about this play, I thought.

Johnson carried the ball toward the line of scrimmage, stopped right before he crossed it, and threw a screen back to me. But it was a lousy pass. I gave it my star Q.B.-all, but the ball landed in back of me and bounced away.

As I scrambled for it, I managed a quick glance at Billy Bob, lumbering down the field. Nobody picked him up. Nobody thought they needed to be on him. That was the point. Okay. Maybe this play wasn't lost, yet. I grabbed the pigskin and the Dummy-D rushers were on me. I dodged left, then right. I managed to evade them. I set and threw. Straight to Billy Bob.

But he never even turned around. I watched with pure frustration as the ball hit him smack on the back of the helmet. Kilmer's screech of a whistle split the cool air. Some of the early morning spectators were laughing out loud. My father looked furious.

Kilmer stormed toward me. "When'd the damn circus come to town?"

Why hadn't Billy Bob just turned around to see the ball? It was too simple. "Woulda been six if he'd shown his numbers," I defended myself.

"For which team?" the coach thundered. "Listen hard, boy. You stick to basics. We're a runnin' team. Hear me?" He grabbed my face mask and I flinched. "You only call the plays I tell you to. Got that? You're the god-damned dumbest smart kid I know."

Smart kid? Shit, that was as close to a compliment the coach had ever paid me.

But I wasn't the only one to earn his wrath. I

overheard him bawling Billy Bob out near the locker rooms after practice. I was spying, actually. After the whole business with Lance's knee, there was no way I was gonna trust the guy as far as I could throw him. I hung back in the hallway, just around the corner where the coach had Billy Bob up against the wall.

"You're draggin' ass out there, and it's fuckin' up my universe," Coach Kilmer spat. "You understand me? You're fat, you're slow, and all of a sudden you're lazy. And if it wasn't for you I would still have my startin' quarterback. I'm just wonderin' what happened to you."

I could imagine Billy Bob quivering like three hundred pounds of Jell-O. "Coach . . ." I heard him whimper.

"I don't want excuses. I want you to fix it."

Billy Bob didn't respond. I figure he was working his mouth, struggling to come up with what to say, but failing.

"Get the fuck outta here!" Kilmer howled at him.

I had no doubt that Billy Bob took the opportunity to do just that.

Darcy's butt wiggled up and down as she walked across the school parking lot. Okay, I was staring. Guilty as charged. But it was kinda hard not to when all that was covering it was a pair of barely there, cut-off denims, with the words "Beat Em" spelled out right across the sweetcheeks. And I do mean sweet. "Beat" on one cheek, "Em" on the other.

She must have felt my eyes on her. She turned, struck a pinup worthy pose, and waited for me to catch up to her. "What time, Mox?" she asked, showing me her pearly whites.

"What time what?"

"What time you comin' over tonight?"

"Tonight?" Was I missing something here? No, actually I caught her drift perfectly.

"It's half price night at the gun club," she said. "My parents never get home before twelve."

But wasn't she managing to forget about someone? Someone with whom she'd been experiencing the joys of the wash cycle a few weeks ago? "I went to see Lance today at the—"

"This is about you and me," she interrupted me. "I've known you my whole life. I'm not tellin' anyone you're comin' over. Anytime after seven." Like a royal requesting an audience, she left no room for discussion. It was a date.

Speechless, I watched her walk away, the message on her perfect butt undulating sexily.

Kyle and I cruised the mini-mart, scoring a post-dinner snack. My brother wore a small fez—you know, one of those little pillbox shaped African hats? The fez was yellow, red and green—the colors of black pride, of African-American consciousness-raising. A severe black suit completed his look as a member of the Fruit of Islam. I didn't have the heart to tell him he was several dozen shades too pasty and pale for his outfit. Moving on from the Zen master . . .

As I passed the glass doors of the beer cooler, I stopped and checked out the sexy, bikini-clad babe on the beer ad hanging on the wall next to the cooler. Cute. Beautiful, even. And oozing sex appeal. But no more than Darcy did. I addressed the poster. "Why be good? I'm always good. What's the upside of my being good?"

More temptation at the check-out counter: a shelf sporting every possible variety of condom—ribbed, smooth, nibbed, nubbed. Lubricated, flavored, glow-in-the-dark. *Extra-sensitive*. Jesus, a guy could be excused for thinking that the message here was "Just say yes." My gaze rocketed around the mini-mart. The magazine rack—babes with barely anything on. The wall above the register—a calendar featuring the pom-pom girls of our state's own Dallas Cowboys. And those beer babes, inviting you to have more than just a cold one. I gritted my teeth.

Kyle stood next to me at the check-out counter, back straight, face serious. "I'm eighteen. C'mon, it wouldn't be my fault!" I said. "Variety is the spice of life. She invited me over. I'm just bein' polite! Right! Kyle?!"

Kyle stared straight at me.

"Kyle??"

"I only answer to one name," he said. "I am The Honorable El Ali Akbar Shabazz Da."

"That's a bunch of names," I told him.

He ignored me. "There's one God, all praise be to Allah."

"Yeah, but would Allah nail Darcy if he had the chance, huh? Huh? I think so," I said. I grabbed the extra-sensitive condoms—two packs, just to be on the safe side—and put them on the counter. An ebony-skinned clerk with a mild manner rang up our purchases.

"As . . . Salaam . . . Alaikum," Kyle said to him. He looked at Kyle and furrowed his brow.

"Um, that'll be ten eighty-nine altogether," he said.

I paid for everything, and put the rubbers in my wallet.

Darcy lived in a large, two-floor house, white with black trim, a spacious veranda, and these big pillars flanking the heavy, shiny wood door. Neo-colonial, I think they call it. The lawn was broad, its boundaries marked by high hedges, with a weeping willow standing guard.

It's not that I'm some kind of Architectural Digest freak. It's just that I had plenty of time to notice all this, because it was the wait of a lifetime. My hands felt clammy, despite the cool night breeze, and my heart beat fast and guiltily and excitedly. But no one answered the doorbell, even though there were a few lights on inside.

I was on the verge of going back down the slate-flagged front walk, when the porch light went on and the heavy door opened. Darcy had on a pair of blue sweats and a white T-shirt. Her hair hung loosely around her face. Her skin was clear and luminous. She wore no make-up. She looked absolutely beautiful.

"I gave up on you," she said, without a hello.

"Is it too late?" I asked. I wasn't a hundred percent sure if I wanted her to say yes or no.

"No, come on in."

I followed her inside. The click of the door closing behind us was decisive. I had made up my mind. We traded a little chit-chat. How're you doing—that kind of thing. But we both knew why I was here. Darcy took my hand. I felt my pulse kick into overdrive. She led me down to the family room in the basement—a large, rug-covered room, with a big-screen TV, a good stereo system, and some comfortable sofas. I'd been here plenty of times with Lance. I'd even been here with my mom when Darcy and I were little. But this was a whole different story.

"I'm glad you came," Darcy said. "I mean, it's kinda weird to have you in my house. Isn't it?"

"Yeah, I feel like I'm doing something illegal."

"Well, not yet," Darcy said lightly. We laughed nervously. "Umh, look at me. I'm a mess," she added. "No one ever sees me like this."

It was true that I hadn't seen Darcy dressed down in years. But it suited her well. "This is the best I've seen you look," I told her sincerely.

Her face lit up in a gratifying smile. "You're sweet, Mox. But you know you are. Listen, I was about to make an ice cream sundae. You want one?"

"Umh . . ." I wanted something so bad I could almost taste it. But it wasn't an ice cream sundae I was craving.

"Yeah, have one. I'll make it," Darcy insisted. "Do you want whipped cream?"

What the hell. Who could say no to an ice cream sundae? And Darcy seemed so excited about it. "Sure," I said. "Whipped cream would be good."

Darcy did a 180 and rolled out of the room. My eyes followed every step. Yeow, the girl knew how to use her body. *Be still my beating heart.* I took a few long, deep breaths to try to slow my pulse, but it was absolutely no use. There was no getting around the fact that my being here was not really in the good and right-eous boy's book of rules. And that made the whole thing even more exciting.

Some slow, sexy, vaguely familiar song was slithering out of the stereo speakers. My head spun. I swayed to the mellow, seductive melody. Every nerve of my body was on alert. I tugged at my sweater and ran a hand through my hair.

—I halted, slack-jawed, as Darcy came back in. Oh, my god. She was completely naked, except for a whipped cream bikini, covering only the bare essentials. Two cherries decorated the tips of her whipped cream covered breasts.

"C'mere," she said softly.

My feet just sort of started moving toward her. It was like I was hypnotized. Lost. She was the most delicious looking ice cream sundae I'd ever seen. I could almost taste the sweetness of a kiss mixed with whipped cream. I reached out toward her. Her arms went around my shoulders as I took her face in my hands. Her skin was warm. Our lips parted. Our mouths met, soft and wet and—

"No." I pulled back. "I can't. We can't. It's just . . . not, no." I stepped away from her. "No! I'm sorry."

"What?" Darcy's pretty face creased in shock and dismay. "You're sorry?"

There was a small blanket on one of the sofas. I handed it to her. I couldn't look at the whipped cream bikini and still do the valiant thing for very long. "There's Lance and Jules," I said, as she grasped the blanket to her body. "I don't know if I love Jules I mean but I might and I know I don't love you and Lance I mean he might love you . . ." My words piled out one on top of another in a light-headed jumble. "Y'know?" I finished lamely.

Darcy's lower lip trembled. Her blue eyes filled with unshed tears. She was as fragile and lovely as I'd ever seen her. "I don't love Lance." The tears spilled forth, rolling down her pink cheeks. "It was never about love. It was about me gettin' a better life. Lance and I were gonna leave. Now I know he's gonna probably stay in West Canaan and be a manager at Wal-Mart and coach J.V. football."

"Darcy," I said. I couldn't really blame her for wanting to get out of West Canaan.

"You're sweet, Mox," she said, wiping her tears away with the blanket. "But I don't love you, either. I just wanted to go with you."

I took the blanket out of her hands and helped her wrap it around herself. "Darcy, you're smart. You'll get outta West Canaan on your own," I said. Wouldn't that be better than riding Lance's coattails to wherever? Or mine? I hugged her to me and we swayed gently to the music.

"Unbelievable," I said, after a little while.

She'd stopped crying. She was breathing evenly. "What?" she asked.

"I usually fall for the whipped cream bikini every time."

Darcy laughed. A real laugh. It was going to be okay between us. I'd known her for way too long for it not to be.

9

Everyone was keyed-up about taking on the Elwood Wildcats. They had an awesome defense, and we'd lost to them before. As if to pound home the severity of the situation, our last practice before we played them took place on a bitter cold morning.

Only a couple of the most die-hard Dads were out there watching, and the steam rising from their coffee cups quickly disappeared as the coffee grew cold before they'd finished it.

Out on the field, we jogged in place, rubbing our hands briskly, trying to keep from freezing. On a day like this, even Kilmer's Navy Seal–level workout was more appealing than standing still.

We were in the middle of a passing drill, my arm half cocked and ready to throw to Tweeder, when he just stopped in his tracks, staring at something behind me. I whirled around. Lance! He hobbled onto the field on his crutches, one pant leg split open wide to accommodate all that machinery on his leg.

I jogged over to him. "They got you up 'n' around, huh?" I asked easily, not wanting to get too heavy and bum him out even more.

But Lance was all business. "Lemme see that ball," he said.

I hesitated. The guy was in no shape to walk, let alone throw a football.

"There's nothing wrong with my arm!" Lance screamed. "Give me the damned thing!"

I looked over at Coach Bates. He shrugged. I looked back at Lance. The poor bastard wanted that ball so bad. I tossed it to him—gently.

Lance let one crutch flop to the ground, leaning heavily on the other as he managed to snag the ball. He stumbled, only barely keeping his footing. Then he set himself. Or some approximation of it—one good leg, one crutch, his useless leg hovering above the ground in plaster and steel.

The whole team was staring at him.

"Well?" he yelled. "What're you waitin' for? Hustle! Z-out left!"

I hurt for the guy. Damn, was he really dying to throw the ball that badly? "Give the man what he wants," I called out sympathetically.

"That's right," Lance said through gritted teeth.

Tad McNurty darted downfield. Lance tucked the one crutch under his armpit and braced himself on it. Tad turned. Lance cocked his arm back—and staggered. His crutch went out from underneath him. He waved his arms wildly, trying to balance on one leg, but he was going, going . . . gone, down on the ground, clutching the football like a teddy bear.

There was nothing funny about it. Lance was dead serious. I'm sure every guy on the field could feel his bitterness and frustration. I know I could. The guy was struggling to get off the ground. I went over to give him a hand.

Lance shook my hand off him. "Leave me be!" he snapped. "I don't need your help."

I stepped back. I saw Coach Kilmer crossing the field toward us.

"Just off-balance," Lance said, wriggling over to reclaim one crutch, then the other. "Lemme try again," he said.

"Lance—"

"Lemme try again!" he demanded. Somehow, he managed to get himself up again, the football tucked under his arm against his body.

"C'mon, Lance," I said gently. "You should take it easy."

The guys were all staring at him with embarrassment. "Get downfield, dammit!" Lance raged.

Johnson, our new frosh receiver, was the only one who moved, dutifully trotting downfield. Lance got the throw off this time, but the ball went a couple of feet and then flopped on the ground. The team was coming over now, gathering around him. Coach Kilmer was at his side. Someone shagged the football and handed it to me.

"Another football!" Lance ordered. He reached out to wrestle the ball away from me. I handed it over. I didn't want to see him go down again.

"Son," Kilmer said matter-of-factly, "we gotta keep the practice goin'."

"Whadaya think I'm doing?" Lance raved at him. I'd never heard him wail on the coach like that. "Run, dammit!" he yelled to Johnson. "Go deep!"

Johnson did a half-hearted jog about midway down the field from us. "Deep!" Lance yelled. "I said go deep!" He got off a feeble pass. The ball left his hands and he started to fall again. I got him in a kind of hug and kept him upright.

"Let go o' me!" he ranted, trying to twist his

way out of my grasp. "Let go! I'm the quarter-back!" His voice broke. I felt him convulsing with silent sobs.

I positioned his crutches for him and helped him find his balance. He hung his head, but I knew he was crying. Kilmer patted him on the back. "Easy, son, easy," he said.

"I'm still the quarterback . . ." Lance said piti-fully. "I'm still the quarterback . . ."

We had to do something to raise Lance's spir-its. I mean, I know some people had abandoned him—taken his picture down, stopped taking the long route past his house, whatever. But Lance was our friend. It was our duty to cheer him up. And I had an idea about how we could do it.

I snagged Wendell by the lockers. "Wendell, we're meetin' at the mini-mart at ten tonight," I said.

Wendell shut his locker and gave the dial of his combination lock a spin. "Ten o'clock? For what?"

I didn't want to leak the surprise. Let 'em all wonder. It would just make it more fun. "Can't tell ya now, but I can't find Billy Bob." I'd been looking for him all morning. A guy that size—he's usually kind of easy to spot. But Billy Bob had been layin' real low. "Something's going down with him."

Wendell shrugged. "Kilmer," he said.

"Kilmer?"

"Yeah, he's staying out of the coach's way. C'mon, man, Kilmer's a fucking racist-ass redneck."

Well, Wendell didn't have to sell me on that. I knew what the guy was. But I'd never heard Wendell trash him like that. "Whoa, this is new," I said.

"Bullshit, Mox. He's been ridin' the fuck out of Billy Bob. Blamin' him for Lance's knee and shit. Look, I'm just over his shit."

"I hear you, man." I guess everyone had reached their limit with that bastard.

But Wendell turned his ire on me. "You *don't* hear me, man. You know how many yards I average a game?"

"A hundred?" I estimated. What was up with Wendell?

"A hundred thirty-three," Wendell said harshly. "Y'know how many touchdowns I have? Huh?"

Oh. Now I saw what he was getting at. I was afraid to guess. A guy who averages 133 yards a game oughta cross the goal line plenty.

"Three." Wendell answered his own question. "And I only got those because I broke for more than twenty yards each time. When we get inside the ten, he calls a sweep for Lance or some fuckin' rollout for a white receiver. It's bullshit. My knees are shot, I've run my ass into the fuckin' ground and you'd think he'd throw me a short T.D. here or there. Bullshit, man."

I let Wendell rail. He had a right to. We all did. I guess I just didn't realize there were other guys—my own pals—who despised Kilmer quite as much as I did. I mean, to most people, he was God. "Fuckin' Kilmer," I sympathized.

Wendell wasn't finished. "You'd think he'd pick up the phone to call A&M or Texas Tech for me? Fuck no. My mom's been doin' all my recruiting. She's got Grambling comin' to see me. Damn, Mox, it's just fucked up."

"Fuck Kilmer, okay? I'll get you into the end zone," I said to Wendell. When I'd stepped up to Lance's job on the field, I'd told myself I was gonna do it for myself. Not for Kilmer. For me. Now I saw that I had to do it for my teammates, too.

Wendell and I shook hands. I pulled him toward me and our handshake turned into a hug. It was all about sticking together. The real meaning of teamwork.

Wendell let go of me, and I saw that Darcy was coming over. She of the whipped cream bikini. I was afraid I might be blushing. Wendell looked at her, then at me. "So we're cool, Mox.

You got shit to tend to. I'll see you at practice."
He strode off down the hall.

Darcy leaned against the locker bank. We traded embarrassed smiles. "Tell me not to feel weird around you," she said.

I tried to push away the image of the whipped cream. The cherries. I looked at her—fully clothed. Well, as clothed as Darcy ever got. Her short, pleated skirt and tight sweater hugged her curves. But her pretty face wasn't so different from the way she'd looked when we were little—when our moms used to make play dates for us to get down and dirty in the sandbox. Thinking about that helped. "Please, Darcy, the last thing I need is anything comin' between us," I said. "We're closer, now. We're friends."

She smiled more confidently. "Yeah, we are. Good." The sound of the bell echoed through the halls. "Thanks, Mox." She leaned up and kissed me. Mouth to mouth. She let her lips linger a little longer than necessary. I let her lips linger a little longer than necessary.

I watched her sashay on down the hall. I grinned.

The grin froze on my face as I turned to see Julie watching me. She stood by the end of the bank of lockers. Her eyes said it all. She'd seen everything. She spun on her heel, and took off in the opposite direction from Darcy.

"Jules!" I called. "Aw, shit. Jules!"

The late bell rang. I quickly got my books out of my locker and hurried toward class. Dammit. It wasn't fair. How many guys would have resisted Darcy Sears in her whipped cream bikini? I had, but I was in major trouble anyway.

Tweeder and I stood side-by-side at the sinks in the school bathroom. In the mirror, I watched him shake a couple of pills out of a prescription vial and pop them into his mouth. He swallowed them without water—a seasoned pro.

I'd been filling him in on the whole Julie thing. Darcy's ice cream sundae, the kiss by the lockers, the way Jules had gotten the wrong idea. Tweeder thought I was nuts for passing on Darcy. And okay, he made me feel kind of virtuous and upright. Maybe that was why I was telling him. But he didn't get it. I don't know why I'd thought he might.

Julie had been giving me the old slip all day. I couldn't even get close enough to her to talk to her. Every time she saw me coming, she'd book. Would've made an excellent quarterback the way she ran, dodging the guy who was on her.

"Bitches, man. I'm telling you," Tweeder said. He did another pill. And one for good luck?

I pulled down a paper towel and dried my hands. I knew Tweeder was trying to commiserate, but calling Julie names didn't really sit so well with me. "Panty droppers," he added.

"What?" I guess I deserved this, confiding in Tweeder about affairs of the heart.

"Give 'em two Vicodins, a Percocet and two beers," Tweeder said. "The panties drop. It's *nice!*"

"It's *nice!*?" Jesus. I had to hope Tweeder was just talking big.

"It's *niiiice!*" Tweeder repeated, pumping his arm for emphasis. Just in case he hadn't gotten his point across.

"You think you'll enjoy prison?" I asked him, deadpan.

That got him. He looked totally confused. Genuinely innocent. "I dunno? What? Wait, where we goin' tonight?"

I laughed. I think Tweeder had some deluded flash that I was taking him to jail tonight. "It's a surprise," I said. "Just make sure everyone meets at the mini-mart at ten, okay?"

"Niiiice," Tweeder said again.

I shook my head. The guy was seriously medicated.

Three nights a week, Julie worked the pickup window at Mr. Freeze. Mr. Freeze had been around forever. My dad and Joe Harbor and their team used to chow down on burgers and chocolate freezes after practice even back when they were Kilmer's Coyotes. The place hadn't changed much. Maybe a fresh coat of paint on the modest white shack every once in a while, and the addition of a chicken burger that registered only 5 on a cholesterol scale of 1 to 10, as opposed to Mr. Freeze's standard 10 on most things.

But the food was filling and cheap, and the fries were good. Julie worked the microphone, letting customers know their orders were ready. Of course Lance never had to work after school—being star Q.B. was a big enough job. But Julie didn't complain about it. On the other hand, it didn't make her love football any better.

I approached the pickup window nervously. I'd put on my cords and a button-down shirt for the occasion. Maybe she'd notice the effort and cut me a little break. She watched me coming through the window. I smiled. She didn't.

"Oh, my god," she said, without any emotion. "It's star quarterback Johnnie Moxon. Somebody hold me up."

I took a deep breath. "Listen, there is nothing going on with Darcy Sears. I've known her since kindergarten. Nothing's ever—"

"You mean you've never seen her in her

whipped cream bikini?" Julie cut me off by firing the question.

Jesus. How did she know? I was stuck for a second. Then I managed a forced laugh. "Whipped cream bikini? No. Absolutely not."

"Funny," Julie said. But she wasn't laughing. "That's how she got Lance."

I didn't doubt it. That's how she could have gotten just about anyone. But not me. Because I was with Julie. At least I had been. "C'mon, Jules. Are we together, or what?"

"I don't date football players," she stated flatly.

She didn't? "But I've always been a football player." I stated the obvious.

"Nah, you were something different. Or at least I thought you were."

She might as well have slapped me. Her words stung. Had I really been acting so different since Lance had gotten hurt? I was just enjoying what I'd never been able to enjoy before. I'd spent my whole life practicing to play football. And now I was playing it. And people appreciated me. And I appreciated *that*. But I was the same person. Wasn't I? It was everyone else who was treating me differently. Including Jules. She should have been too smart for that. Of course, she *had* seen me kissing Darcy at the lockers. Even though it wasn't what she thought. My mind spun.

"What a Kodak moment," Julie said coldly. "Star quarterback John Moxon having a 'gut check' minute about who he really is."

She wasn't being fair. She wasn't even listening. "You don't think all this is hard?" I defended myself.

"Hard? On who?"

"Jules—"

"Mox, we had a thing and it was great. Things have changed a little bit. And that's okay. Maybe I was wrong. You should go." Her voice went from hard to wobbly. I felt myself kind of choking up, too. Was she telling me it was over between us?

"Jules, you can't make me leave," I said.

Julie's answer was to grab the pick-up window microphone. "Oh my god," she squealed into it, making her voice all high and excited. "Everybody come meet Johnnie Moxon—the Mox—the star quarterback of the Coyotes. He's at my window!!"

I reached in and tried to grab the mike, but the damage had been done. A swarm of Coyote fans rushed me and got me surrounded. I couldn't believe this. You know those clips of rock stars being mobbed? It was kind of like that. Young girls looking starry-eyed at me, boys who wanted to grow up to be like me, their dads who remembered their glory days themselves—people of every age and type, with one thing in common. Football.

I looked at Jules as people swarmed around me. She was the only one who didn't love me right at that moment. I broke through the crowd and made a getaway to the Moxmobile.

10

The neon sign read TOPLESS, and it flashed over a picture of an elegant man in a tuxedo taking off his top hat. But nobody was in the dark about the kind of top they really meant. Not even Tweeder or Billy Bob.

I threw the Moxmobile into park, and the posse piled out. "Whee-o!" Tweeder declared gleefully. Wendell just grinned, and Billy Bob stared, open-mouthed, at the low, adobe-style building. I came around to the passenger side and helped Lance get out of the car.

Billy Bob noticed and immediately gave us another hand. "Lance, I'm glad you came," he said. Lance was still his hero. You had to love the guy for that.

Lance was the only one who didn't look psyched for our little night out. "I was kidnapped," he said.

Billy Bob and I set him up on his crutches, and I clapped him on the shoulder. "No crab apples, tonight," I said. "This has been a hard coupla weeks. Lance, you've been cooped up and Kilmer's been kicking our ass. We deserve this." I motioned to the adobe building. "Gentlemen, my gift to you."

"Wait. How the hell we gonna get in?" Wendell frowned.

"I went to football camp with the bouncer," I explained.

Wendell's grin reappeared instantly. We wasted no time heading for the door.

Inside, the smallish room was lit a deep red, with rocket-shaped white lamps glowing on every table. A long, wooden bar stretched along one side of the room, and a low stage was built on another. The place looked like the bastard child of a Country Western bar and a brothel. I mean, not that I've ever been in the second of those two establishments, but in my imagination, this place and that place bore some resemblance.

We were greeted just inside the door by Brett Landon, a refrigerator-sized linebacker. Or ex-linebacker. Brett had retired a number of years ago, after high school, when a collision on the field did an irreversible number on his back. We slapped hello and I introduced everyone around. In the red light of the room, Brett took in Lance's cast. I thought I saw a flicker of recognition in his eyes, but he was cool. "Hey, I read that you guys are undefeated," he said enthusiastically. "That's great."

He waved us through and signaled to a curvaceous woman in a midriff-baring top, microscopic skirt, and cowboy boots. "This is Minnie," he introduced us. Well, her skirt was mini, that was for sure. But certain other things weren't. Minnie led us to a big table with a front and center view of the stage, her butt rolling lusciously as she walked. Uh-huh—we had ourselves a nice little evening going here.

We sat down and she took our drink orders. Our eyes followed her as she headed toward the bar. "Billy Bob, wipe the drool off your mouth," Tweeder said, drooling. Wendell and I traded grins. Lance's mouth was still set tightly, but he watched Minnie's rear end, same as the rest of us.

There was a decent crowd in the club for a weekday. Well, if you consider Thursday a weekday. A lot of people see it as the first day of the weekend. Date night. Party night. Only one day left in the work week night. Whatever. What

I'm trying to say here is that more than half the tables were occupied. A few couples, but mostly guys of all different ages—some alone, some in groups. Add the waitresses in bathing suit–sized outfits, and it made the club feel like a party. Which it was. The music was pumping from the speaker on stage. You could feel the anticipation of the audience.

Minnie was back in a few with shots and beers. "These are from Brett," she said. "You guys are on the house all night."

Cheers and high-fivers from my posse. I reached for a shot and raised the glass. "To Kilmer!" I announced.

The guys raised their glasses. "Fuck Kilmer!" they chorused back resoundingly. I saw Lance smile. Yup. First smile in weeks. Like I said, we had ourselves a nice little evening going here.

"Yo, we've got Elwood tomorrow night," Wendell reminded us. "We can't stay too long." Nothing like someone from within your own ranks to put a damper on things.

"Chill, Wendell," Tweeder said, echoing my sentiments exactly. "Look over your right shoulder."

I looked, too. Jesus F. Christ! A huge, orblike, barely covered pair of breasts were coming right at Wendell and threatening to swallow his head!

He yelped and put his hands up. We all lost it laughing.

The breasts were attached to a dancer in a white, lacy corsetlike thing that tied up the front, but plunged low enough to show off her best assets. She wore a ruffled lace mini-skirted petticoat, a pair of black boots, and in her hand, she carried a staff festooned with ribbons. And just in case anyone—that meant us—was too busy looking at her neckline to get the costume, a slide projector clicked on, and an arc of cuddly, fluffy white sheep appeared on the scrim at the back of the stage.

"Bo Peep does sheep!" Tweeder yelled appreciatively. "Yo, whatcha gonna do with that staff?" The dancer did a little shimmy in front of us, turned around and did another shimmy to showcase her backside, and climbed onto the stage.

We toasted again and downed our beers. A nice little evening. And it was only getting started.

The shots were going down easy. And the beers. And the mixed drinks. As guests of the house, we felt it our obligation to sample from the menu. And they were happy to oblige. When Tweeder started with that "niiiice" deal, I couldn't argue with him this time. I *was* niiiice.

The ladies on stage were niiiice. My buds were niiiice. Even Lance looked like he was feeling pretty niiiice.

Two "cowgirls" had just finished taking their clothes off to some Country and Western, and riding one of those mechanical broncos that they'd dragged onstage. Now, I'll admit, we weren't participating in the most evolved behavior tonight, but what with the liquor flowing and all the tension we needed to release, I was enjoying myself just fine. We're football players, and this is Texas. And once in a while you have to give in to your animal instincts.

Billy Bob was especially good at that. As Brett removed the mechanical bull from the stage, Billy Bob jumped up from the table and started ripping his shirt off.

"Yo, Billy Bob, keep your shirt on!" I said.

Billy Bob pulled his polo shirt over his head and flung it on the floor. "It's a strip club, baby! And I must work," he added, echoing the title of the Ru Paul song pounding out of the speakers between acts.

Billy Bob broke for the stage and scrambled up. He gyrated his hips around like a hula dancer, his massive belly shaking. I hoped he wasn't gonna try to take off his pants.

Brett left the bull on the side of the stage and calmly took Billy Bob by the shoulders. He was way cool about walking Billy Bob back to his seat, and motioning for Minnie to bring him another beer.

Lance was laughing. He smacked me on the back. "Y'know, yer a good friend," he said, his words slurring together slightly. "Don't think I don't purr-reciate that you came and vizitted me in th' hospital."

I smiled. "Cool."

"Thanks for bringin' me out tonight," he went on. "Yer a pal, d'I tell you that?"

The optimistic, enthusiastic Lance was back, the Lance who loved life was back, if only for a drunken night. "You're not gonna hug me, are you?" I asked him.

Minnie appeared and set a beer in front of Billy Bob. Billy Bob shimmied his bare-chested rolls of blubber at her. "Easy, big guy," she said. "Now, let's see." Her eyes did a quick survey of all the drinks on our table. "What else could you possibly need?"

"I'd love a small cup of warm water to soak my nuts in," Lance said.

I cracked up, spewing out a mouthful of beer. Lance cracked up. We cracked up together. The last couple of weeks of weirdness between us disintegrated in a haze of alcohol and scantily clad women. Minnie looked at us like we'd lost it, and walked away.

We were still cracking up as the lights went low. A hush fell over the crowd as if the regulars knew something special was about to happen. We glanced at each other as Van Halen's "Hot For Teacher" began to throb out of the speakers. Slowly—excruciatingly, teasingly slowly—the lights came back up again to reveal an incredibly sexy dancer dressed up as a prim, old-time schoolteacher. She held a pointer in one hand, and in the other, a book raised coyly in front of her face. Only her eyes, behind a pair of cat's-eye glasses, were visible. She wore a long skirt and a high-necked buttoned up shirt—tight enough for us to see that when she took it all off we were in for a treat. Her hair was fastened into a bun.

Something about the teacher thing really did it for us high-school guys, I gotta tell you. I heard Lance let out a low moan. I couldn't have put it better.

Our sex goddess strutted on stage. She swiveled her hips, a smooth, round achingly sensuous motion. She used the pointer to fling loose the ties to her skirt, and it fell around her ankles in a puddle. She stepped out of it with lean, long, gorgeous, black-stockinged legs and a pair of very unschoolmarmish spike heels. The stockings were held up by a pair of black garters. A couple of guys got too close to the stage, wolf whistling at teacher. She shook her pointer at them.

Teacher lady was hot. Our posse hollered their approval.

She turned her back to us and put the pointer on the ground, giving us an incredible view of her ass as she bent down. She stood up and turned back to us, always with the book up, as if no matter how much she took off, she was still a prim schoolteacher, too shy and sweet to show her face.

She unbuttoned her shirt, one lingering button at a time. I held my breath. She worked her way from the top button to the bottom. Finally, her shirt was open. She shrugged out of it. Oh, my god. Sheer black bra, black G-string and black spike heels. And those glasses and book. She came forward to the front of the stage, right in front of our table. She unpinned her bun, and a cascade of soft, strawberry-blonde waves tumbled down around her bare shoulders. She took off her glasses and tossed them away carelessly. She bent down low, giving us the primo view as she unhooked her bra and threw the book away, too.

Yes, I looked at her chest before I looked at her face, or I would have realized a couple of seconds sooner. I couldn't help it. Her breasts were magnificent. And I was drunk. I ogled. An admittedly crude whistle escaped through my teeth. The guys were howling. And then I looked up at her face, and the whistle died instantaneously. The howling stopped just as abruptly. It was slack-jawed silence all around the table. Because we were looking right up into the blue eyes of Miss Davis!

Miss Davis was shocked into paralysis, too. We stared at each other. Horror was written across her pretty face.

I was the first to recover. Why should she be horrified? She had to be the most gorgeous, sexy, luscious teacher ever to step foot into a classroom. I let out another whistle of appreciation. My buds followed suit, clapping and hooting.

Miss Davis recovered. She started moving to the music. The show must go on! And it did— after that staggering moment. She tossed her mane of hair. I guess she realized that what was done was done. Besides, she was the teacher and she was in charge. She picked up the pointer. She did unmentionable things with the pointer. (Hey, a gentleman can't give away every secret.) But I can tell you this—she was definitely, unquestionably, no contest, my favorite teacher.

We emptied all the bills out of our wallets and threw them onstage. Miss Davis tucked them into the tops of her sheer black stockings.

Billy Bob got up and started working the other guys in the club to cough up their money, too. "That's my teacher!" he exclaimed, proudly and drunkenly.

I have to say, he spoke for all of us.

Later—many, many drinks and many lovely ladies later—Miss Davis came out into the club in a silk, leopard-print kimono and joined us at our table. She was shy and hesitant at first, and this time it wasn't even an act. But we drunkenly told her how wonderful and sexy and fabulous she was. Well, all of us except Wendell did. Wendell had passed out a couple of rounds ago, and was sound asleep with his head on the table.

"No, it was stylish," Tweeder told our teacher. "Topical, erotic and fun. I gave it a nine-point-five."

Billy Bob raised his hand.

"Yes, Billy Bob?" Miss Davis said.

"Ten. A fucking ten," he said eagerly. He held his hands in front of himself like giant boobs. "You've got fucking Guns of Navarone, and ass. You've got—" He stood and grabbed his own huge ass. "Ass! You've got ass forever!" He stumbled backwards and went right down to the floor, still clutching his ass.

He made no attempt to get up right away.

Lance was more circumspect. He was just as fucked up as the rest of us, but he used his usual line. "I love you, Sister. Can I hug you?" he asked. He leaned over to Miss Davis and gave her a sincere, respectful, drunken hug.

When he let go, I added my compliments. "You're the coolest fuckin' teacher in the universe. And that's not just 'cause I've seen you naked."

I picked up a shot glass and made my hundredth or so toast of the evening. "To Miss Davis," I said.

"To Miss Davis," my friends agreed. Well, not Wendell 'cause he was asleep, and not Billy Bob 'cause he was on the floor, but they would have agreed with me if they could have.

The light of the dawning day was painful. We stumbled out into the parking lot, blinking and holding our hands up to our eyes and groaning. I looked around at our little team. We looked like shit. No way around it. Red-eyed, staggering, oozing the smell of booze from every pore. Only Wendell was anywhere close to semi-steady, having slept in the club for the past three hours. He held Lance under the arm, half carrying, half dragging him toward the Moxmobile. I opened the back door, and he put Lance inside, careful even in this drunken state to watch out for his leg.

My head reeled. The ground seemed to be moving, undulating, spinning. "I can't drive," I said.

"Drive," Billy Bob grunted. "I."

I looked at him. All three of him, from my perspective, and that's a lot of Billy Bob. "Did you just say 'Drive I'?"

He nodded yes.

"You can't speak," I noted.

He shook his head. "Speak. No."

"But you think you should drive."

He nodded yes, again.

"Well, I'm good with that," I said sarcastically. "You don't need to speak to drive. Anyone else?" The rest of them were piling into the car. "Wait! You're gonna get in a car with Native-American Bob? The fat Indian? Have you heard him try to speak? 'Drive I. Speak no. Me drive car. Kill everyone.' He's Chief Running Vomit and you're all ready to get in a car with him."

"I'll drive," volunteered Tweeder. "I'm okay. I mean, I did throw up more than you guys." Jesus. That really inspired confidence, didn't it?

"I'm not drunk," Wendell said. "I guess I must've slept it off." He sounded alright, actually. At least to my wasted ears. I mean, I don't think all that liquor could have left his system entirely, but it was as good as we were going to get. I threw Wendell my car keys—a bum pass

153

but he caught them anyway. A positive sign. I had to go with it. Otherwise we were going to have to sleep in the parking lot.

We almost got home without any trouble. Almost. Wendell's driving wasn't the problem. He did just fine. He held the road all the way back to West Canaan. We were all already dreaming about getting horizontal in a nice, warm bed, getting a few hours of shut-eye before school, and not having to even attempt to function for a while. I for one intended to get Kyle to tell Mom and Dad that I was feeling a little under the weather this morning and that I was going to sleep in, to rest up for the game tonight. Now that I was starting Q.B., I didn't think they'd give me a hard time about that. Man, that bed was going to feel great—

Jesus! Suddenly the wail of a siren made its way through the fog in my brain. From my passenger side seat, I glanced in the rearview mirror. Flashing lights! A police car bearing down on us.

"What the—aw, shit," Wendell said, heeding their signal to pull over.

"Whad'ja do?" Lance asked drunkenly. The patrol car pulled up behind us, and two troopers got out.

"Whoops!" Tweeder said, laughing. "We are in some deep, serious shit here."

"Why? I didn't do anything," Wendell insisted.

I remembered the broken taillight I hadn't gotten fixed yet.

One of the State Troopers stuck his head in through the driver's side. He looked around at us and a huge grin spread across his face. "Mornin' boys," he said.

His partner's face appeared next to his. "Think the coach's gonna bail ya outta this one?" He had on the ol' happy face, too. Was there some joke I wasn't getting?

"You wanna see my license?" Wendell asked. "I'm not drunk."

"Turn the car off and give me the keys," said the first trooper. Why did these guys looks so familiar?

It hit me just as Tweeder leaned up from the back seat. He was still laughing. Apparently he was in on the joke, too. "Hey! It's the mount-me guys!" He greeted them like they were pals of his. "You're not still pissed about the car, are ya?"

Well, he was right about one thing. We were in some deep, serious shit. The broken taillight was the least of our worries.

We dragged our sorry asses down the road. You know how they talk about walking it off?

The troopers decided to make it so. Except that after mile after miserable mile, we were still drunk. We wove along the shoulder of Route 1, past the mall, everything still locked up tight, only a few delivery trucks making early morning drop-offs before the stores opened. My head pounded, and I was dizzy and nauseous.

"It's more than three more miles," I groaned. The sun was coming up way too fast for me, and though it warmed up my icy hands, it made my head hurt worse.

"Least they took Lance," Tweeder said.

"At least," I muttered. Lance's knee made him the lucky one this morning.

11

Rodriguez, our center, snapped me the ball. I rolled out. Or tried to. Before I'd even made a commitment to go left or right, three of Elwood's most monstrous were on top of me. I got the wind knocked out of me as they smashed me against the turf. My head felt like it had cracked in two inside my helmet. Of course, it hadn't felt too great before they'd tackled me, either.

Our night out wasn't helping in the field, that was for sure. If we were playing like shit, it was probably because we felt like shit. But man, you'd think my offensive line could at least *try* to keep me from being creamed like spinach.

The monstrous trio finally piled off me. Everything ached. I lay in a crumpled heap, trying to psych myself to get up. So I could get pounded all over again.

We went into a huddle. I looked around at the guys who were supposed to be protecting me. My left hip and shoulder were throbbing with pain after my most recent experience at the literal bottom of the heap. "You guys wanna try to stop these guys from planting my ass?" I asked angrily.

"I got the squirts, Mox," Billy Bob said. Well, thank you for sharing that with me, Billy Bob. "That liquor's still in my system," he added.

"Me too, man," Tweeder said. "My head feels like I'm under water. I just keep seein' Miss Davis's ass like it's throbbin' on my head and—"

"I'm hung over, too." I cut him off. "But we gotta get on the board. Alright, package four. Tweeder, you Z-out. Collins, run like hell. On one." The word "one" was barely out of my mouth when Elwood started their monster blitz again. I was a second away from sucking more dirt. But somehow our line managed to keep them off me this time.

With half the Elwood D trying to get at me, Tweeder was wide open. I fired downfield.

Call it a little too much enthusiasm. Call it a lot too hung over. Call it both. I knew as soon as the ball left my hands that the pass blew. Not that I had a chance to see where it landed. I was buried under three Elwood defenders, just praying for them to get their knees out of my face. And then I heard them booing me. My own fans. Those loyal Coyote boosters, who'd followed us all the way to Elwood, actually booed me as I lay on the ground. Let me tell you, that is not a good feeling. Isn't there an expression, don't boo a guy when he's down?

Hard to believe it was possible, but things actually managed to go downhill from there. My passing didn't improve. My head didn't stop pounding. Elwood dished out one violent hit after another, leaving us hurt and exhausted and caked with mud. Tweeder dropped a ball that hit him right between the numbers—an impossible pass to miss, but he missed it. Billy Bob made a quick detour during a time out to worship at the altar of the porcelain goddess.

By the third quarter, all I could pray for was that it would be over mercifully soon. Kilmer? You can imagine the intensity of his rage. He'd started out bellowing and threatening and mocking. By this point in the game he was stone cold silent. He radiated fury. I couldn't even look at him. Nor my dad and mom, up there in the bleachers.

I gritted my teeth as I took the next snap. BOOM! I was hit. I must have blacked out for a few seconds. They say a guy who's been tackled can suffer the impact of a major car accident. But the guy in a car accident doesn't have to get right up and charge into another accident. I lay on my back. I couldn't get a breath. I tried to move my legs, but they didn't respond. Panic took hold of me.

My teammates swarmed around me, staring down at me with worry. *Move, damn it*, I told myself. I got an arm braced against the ground and pushed myself up onto one elbow. I saw my mother, on her feet in the bleachers. Darcy had dropped her pom-poms, hands to her mouth in alarm. With supreme effort, I got to my knees. Then to my feet. There was a smattering of applause. Sure felt better than being booed.

Wendell and Tweeder got on either side of me and helped me off the field. My lip was split. I could taste the blood running into my mouth. But I barely had taken a couple of breaths before I was going back into the game.

About all we were able to rack up in the next quarter were a pile of bloody towels and one measly, pitiful field goal. I'll spare you the pathetic details. With the clock running down, and my team desperate to get as far off the field as possible, I felt a sudden surge of disgust. At my team. At me. Those fans booing? We deserved it. And maybe that was exactly what I needed to motivate me. Suddenly, I was barking signals like my life depended on it. I took the snap and faded back like it all mattered. I looked to the end zone and saw that Wendell had a step on his defender. Maybe there was no way to save this game, but I wasn't going down without a good fight. I drew my arm back and unleashed a gorgeous spiral. I watched it zoom, soar . . . right into the hands of the Elwood free safety!

I burned with humiliation as the Elwood fans went wild. We had no way to stop the clock. The Coyotes's fans were filing out of the stadium in dejected, angry droves. I made my way off the field as Elwood kneeled on the ball to end the game.

It was over. It had been a massacre. We were lucky we'd been left standing.

I thought that Coach Kilmer might finish whatever damage Elwood had left undone. I thought he might explode, go off, throttle someone to death. That someone being me.

But even more terrifying, Kilmer was absolutely calm. In control. Yea though he walked through the locker room of the shadow of death, he did not yell. He did not grimace. He did not betray a single shred of emotion.

We answered his silence with silence. We were petrified. We were mortified. The coach circulated through the locker room looking at us emotionlessly. Finally, he spoke. His voice was soft, in command, he ruled, he dominated. He didn't need to yell. "The hard work of so many is sacrificed by the disrespect of a few," he said.

He looked around at all of us, while his words sunk in. I flinched as his gaze came to rest on me. "Moxon, you sacrificed the honor of this football team and the town that supports it." I almost had to strain to hear his words. He laughed, a low, quiet, scary laugh. "Damn, you poisoned my team, son. Hope last night was fun."

Jesus. He knew. There was an unbearable, drawn-out pause. And then he struck, his voice exploding off the hard, shiny surfaces of the locker room. "You think you don't have to listen to me!?" His words were like a fist. "Your dad was a no-talent pussy, but at least he listened!"

I willed myself to meet his seething gaze. What a supreme shit the guy was. Next to me, Billy Bob was sobbing quietly. I looked over at him. He hung his head, trying desperately to swallow his cries. His big body shook.

Certain animals can sniff out the weakest and sickest of their prey and go for the jugular. Kilmer was like that. He whirled on Billy Bob. "Little Billy Bob, crybaby. You cost me my perfect season. How does that feel? Huh? Cry me a river, you fat fucking baby. You disgust me. My star quarterback's draggin' his leg around 'cause of you and on top of it I gotta watch you cry about it? No, y'know what? Get the the fuck outta here. I don't wanna see your fat face! Get out! Get the fuck outta here!"

Billy Bob didn't even attempt to defend himself. Without raising his head, he lumbered out of the locker room, still in his filthy, sweaty uniform.

I thought about surfing the first train outta town for Brazil. If only Jules weren't too pissed to go with me. Or maybe I'd just get into the Moxmobile and head south until I got past the border. Nothing a few dozen shots of Mexican tequila wouldn't cure. Except that after last night, I never wanted to touch another drop of liquor again.

In the end, I drove straight home to get it over with. The *it* being my parents' funerary expressions, the disillusionment on their faces, the displeasure. Mom was buzzing around the kitchen, silently preparing dinner, and Dad was at the kitchen table, just staring at the wall. He started in on me the second I entered the room.

"People are sayin' you organized an all-night drinkin' party. That's why you guys dragged ass out there."

"Save it, Dad," I begged him. I was a hundred-percent beaten and depressed. I still had my wet, smelly, grimy uniform on—having wanted to get the hell out of the locker room and away from Kilmer as soon as was humanly possible. I just wanted to take a shower and then lie down on my bed in the dark with my eyes closed. But my dad wasn't saving anything.

"Excuse me?" he asked, with great umbrage. "Save what? You have the opportunity of a lifetime and you throw it away? It's a joke to you."

"Playing football at West Canaan is *not* the opportunity of a lifetime," I informed him. I was so tired of everyone equating football with life. I was so tired, period. I'd fucked up. I knew it. I felt lousy about it. Could we move on here?

My father's face creased in fury. "Your attitude's wrong, and the tone of voice is wrong. It's an opportunity—"

"For you!" I cut him off. "Playing football at West Canaan could have been the opportunity of *your* lifetime. But I don't want your life!"

My mother brandished the spoon in her hand like a weapon. "Okay, Johnnie, enough! Apologize to your father."

At that moment, Kyle came in through the back door, leading Bacon on a leash. Had he abandoned his religious mania to become a pig farmer now? "What's Bacon doin' here?" I asked.

Kyle shrugged. "Billy Bob dropped him off. Said you'd know to take care of him."

Billy Bob had dropped off his beloved pig? No way. The B-meister wouldn't ever abandon Bacon. They were in it till death did them part. A chill shot up my spine. This could mean only one thing. I raced across the kitchen, burst out the back door and sprinted to the Moxmobile. I prayed I wouldn't be too late.

I looked for him at his house, but no one was home. I looked for him at school. I looked for him in and around the stadium, the mini-mart, the old drive-in lot, where they now had a flea market on the weekend. I drove up and down Main Street. I was getting more and more desperate.

I poured on the speed, screeching through the mall. My breath was coming short and shallow. Billy Bob. My friend since childhood. My friend who'd always been there for me—even when I was second string. My friend who'd learned this damned game right along next to me in the pee-wee league. Billy Bob. He of the big belly and bigger heart—shit, I was composing a eulogy in my head already. Despairing, I drove by the old field where we used to play way back then.

A monster wave of relief washed over me as I spotted his truck in the middle of the field. I made a sharp, noisy turn into the parking lot. Through my windshield, I could see Billy Bob in his cowboy hat, sitting on the tailgate of his truck. Thank God! I turned off my engine, got out of the Moxmobile, and headed over.

BAM! A shotgun blast split the dusk sky. My pulse skipped a horrified beat. I hit the ground, sick with fear. But when I dared to look up, I saw that Billy Bob was still sitting on the back of his truck. Another wave of relief. Jesus, if Billy Bob didn't kill himself, I was going to kill him for scaring me like that. I rushed over to him.

He held a long, polished shotgun. In the back of the truck was a box filled with his football trophies. I saw a few I recognized lying on top. Calmly, he selected a trophy, placed it on the edge of the flatbed, took aim, and then blasted the hell out of it. Brass and wood splintered like shrapnel. He took a long pull from a bottle of Jack Daniels he'd stashed near the trophies. He was so intent on blowing his trophies to smithereens that it took him a few minutes to realize he wasn't alone.

When he finally spotted me, he simply looked at me for a few seconds and then turned back to let another trophy have it right between the eyes.

"Can I—"

"Don't move!" he ordered me. He set up his

next target. "This was for most improved player at linebacker camp when I was eleven." I steeled myself as he blasted the small trophy. "How'd you find me?" he asked without even glancing at me again.

"I drove by every place else in town. This was the only place left."

Billy Bob selected another trophy. "These were our championship trophies from the Steelers. We were nine. Do you remember this shit? Playing peewee?"

I'd just been thinking about it. "Yeah, it was fun," I said.

"No, it wasn't," Billy Bob contradicted me. "I only remember gettin' yelled at." He took another swig of whiskey. He was a bit unsteady as he aimed at the trophy. "You're too fat, Billy Bob!" BOOM! He fired off a shot. "You're too slow and too dumb!" BOOM! BOOM! Another and another. He sat down on the tailgate to reload. "We were little kids, Mox. Little kids. Nothin' was ever good enough."

Poor guy. I couldn't have felt sorrier for him. And I knew what he was talking about, too. It wasn't like I'd ever been good enough. Not with Lance in the game. "It's almost over," I consoled him.

"No, it's over," he said flatly. "It's over." I didn't like the sound of that. It was very . . . final.

"C'mon, man," I said.

"What?" He casually cranked off two rounds from the shotgun. This time, he didn't even bother to set up a trophy. He just shot into the darkening sky.

"This is bullshit," I said gently.

"What?" he asked again.

"You're gonna let this fuckin' football shit get you? Kilmer? You're gonna let Kilmer win?"

"What am I supposed to do?" His voice rose. "Huh? Tell me." He choked a little. I could tell he was about to lose it. And that gun was loaded.

"Quit," I said. "Fuck it. Who cares about Kilmer's twenty-third district championship? I don't." And as I said it, all of a sudden it was true. What the hell was a district championship compared to my friend, sitting here with a shotgun in his hands?

"*I* care about the twenty-third district championship," Billy Bob said. "Coach loved me and treated me like a son." He waved the shotgun at the peewee scoreboard. It was decorated with a poster of Coach Kilmer's face, larger than life. Even on the peewee field, he reigned supreme. "Kilmer told me to protect Lance and I didn't," Billy Bob went on. "I fucked everything up." It was all pouring out now, and Billy Bob was sobbing. But I was angry.

"Kilmer fucked everything up and every

player on that team knows it," I said. I grimaced at the coach's picture.

"Nah, yer wrong about Kilmer, Mox."

I struggled with Billy Bob's warped perception of the coach. You know that syndrome where people who've been kidnapped start to identify with their kidnappers? I think Billy Bob had a variation of that. I tried a different approach. "There's one game left for the district, and we need you," I told him. "I need you. I mean, who the fuck's gonna protect *my* ass?"

Slowly, gently, nonthreateningly, I reached for his gun. Billy Bob pulled it away from me, then looked at me and surrendered it. There was a moment that seemed frozen. Then Billy Bob started laughing. I joined in, laughing from sheer relief. We shook hands. "I'll protect your bony ass," Billy Bob said.

"It's not bony," I protested. "I mean, I think I gotta nice ass."

"It's alright. Your ass, it's niiiice," he said. We busted out laughing.

I aimed the shotgun right at the poster of Kilmer. WELCOME FUTURE COYOTES, the sign read. I cocked the gun. I pressed firmly against the trigger. BOOM! I blasted the picture right off the scoreboard. Damn, that felt good.

Billy Bob howled in approval. I smiled with satisfaction.

12

I helped myself to eggs and sausage and slid into my seat at the table to dig in. I'd gotten a good night of shut-eye, and I was feeling like a human being again. A sore, banged-up loser of a human being after the game we'd played, but still a human being. I said good morning to Mom, and she took the time out from frying a whole bunch of stuff to smile at me, so maybe I was forgiven and we could go on from there.

Dad came in from the living room just as Kyle entered the kitchen through the back door, a parade of—let's see, seven, eight, nine kids—nine kids marching in formation behind him. Right foot, right foot. Left foot, left. They were all dressed in pure white—pants, shirts, tennis shoes.

Dad stared for a second. Okay, we all stared for a second. "What's the deal with these kids?" Dad asked, already annoyed before Kyle had even explained.

"These are my people," Kyle intoned. His "people" nodded solemnly.

"Your people?" Dad thundered.

Mom stopped frying again. "Kyle, did you start a cult?" she asked.

"Yes," Kyle answered.

Mom's brow furrowed for a moment. Then she gave a feeble smile. "That's nice," she said helplessly.

"Out!" Dad roared. "Get them out!" He started pushing Kyle's "people" out the back door. "Freakos! Go home! Get lost!" he screamed.

Kyle watched his flock disappear. Wordlessly, his expression blank, he sat down at his place at the kitchen table. Dad whirled on him. "That's it! No more religions for you! You're healthy and you're gonna play football! You hear me? Huh?"

I felt sorry for my brother. As if football wasn't another religion around here. I changed the subject. "Hey, Dad," I said, oh so casually.

He spun around and looked at me, still angry about Kyle.

"Dad, was that Sheriff Bigelow and Chet

McNurty I saw you talking to out on the lawn just now?" I knew it was. I'd seen them out the bathroom window after my shower, holding some kind of pow-wow with my dad. "What did they want?" I asked breezily.

But I didn't feel breezy. I felt suspicious. All those two men ever seemed to think about was football. At their age. If the sheriff spent as much time on law and order, West Canaan would have one of the world's lowest crime rates. Actually it had a pretty low crime rate. Because everyone was too busy going to football games and watching football on TV and talking football to cause too much trouble. Except for stealing State Troopers' patrol cars from time to time. But I'm getting off the track. I just want you to understand that I knew the sheriff and Mr. McMurty were here talking to my dad about me. And I didn't like it.

Dad kind of hemmed and hawed. "We're all a little worried about Gilroy. That's all," he said.

"It's their first year in our division," I reminded him. Man, I was still recovering from the last game, and already the pressure was mounting about the next one.

"But they played 4-A, last year. Since they dropped to 3-A they been killing people. I'm telling you *hurting* people," my father said. "To be honest, the sheriff said he hopes the Gilroy game doesn't matter. I assured him that you were gonna stick to the plan."

"Yeah, well . . ." I said, uncomfortably.

"Son. Tell me you're gonna stick to the plan," he ordered.

"Fine. I'm gonna stick to the plan," I said without any emotion. "Good," said my father. "That's what I wanted to hear." I nodded. That's why I'd said it.

I scarfed my breakfast quickly and made ready to escape. I grabbed a muffin from the kitchen counter for my ride, and almost made it out the back door.

"Oh, wait, Mox," my father said from the table. "This letter came for you yesterday." He pulled a crisp white envelope out from under his folded up newspaper. I came back in and took it. I scanned the return address.

"Brown!" I felt my heart pound. And the envelope was fat! They said the rejection letters were thin—one page saying thanks but no thanks. The acceptance letters came with all sorts of forms and information. I tore the envelope open.

"Dear Mr. Moxon," I read. "We would like to welcome you to the Brown University Class of 2002." I'd made it! Oh, my god! I was in! And I was out—of West Canaan, that is. Brown! My first choice! I'd done it! I was a college student!

Mom and Kyle let out hoots and hollers. Kyle's pure, white-clad, understated weirdness was shattered. He was up and out of his seat. He was doing a little dance in the middle of the kitchen. He was grabbing me in a bear hug. I grinned. "Kyle, lemme finish the letter, man. We are very pleased to offer you a place . . . blah, blah, blah . . . numerous qualified applicants for each spot . . ." I mumbled, half reading out loud, half reading to myself. "Please contact the financial aid office to discuss the terms of your full academic scholarship." I stopped reading. I was stunned. Full academic scholarship. *Academic*. As in great grades. As in, we think you're a well-rounded, deserving person. As in this is about more than just football. I didn't feel like a loser anymore.

But Dad was still in his seat. "Jonathan, I'm proud about Brown, but I need to finish talking to you about Gilroy." Gilroy? Was I really hearing this? I get into one of the best fuckin' universities in the world—a fuckin' Ivy League—and he's still back in Gilroy, Texas? Talking football? "Gilroy?" I said to him incredulously. "Tell me who wins."

And then I was outta there.

But back in West Canaan High, I was still a loser. Everyone had been to the game and watched me screw up. Everyone. Nobody said anything to me as I walked through the halls. Most of the kids avoided making eye contact. I got to my locker. *Mox Sucks Coyote Ass!* someone had scrawled on it in black magic marker. Well, thank you very much. And okay, maybe I deserved it. Sort of. But what about having fans who stood behind you? What about rallying your team to victory? Whatever. I had my fifteen minutes of fame. Now it was over. B.F.D. This locker was gonna belong to someone else next year anyway. I was college bound. I was a Brown man. The Coyotes were over. Almost.

As I stood staring at the graffiti, Billy Bob plowed into me, almost knocking me over. He had a huge smile on his round face.

"What are you so damn happy about?" I asked. Alright, so I *was* a little irritated about the graffiti. Besides, last time I'd seen Billy Bob, he was shooting his trophies to death.

"My cat's okay!" Billy Bob said exuberantly. "I can play! I took your advice, Mox. They scanned my cat. I'm alright to play."

"Scanned your cat? Oh, you mean your dad took you for a CAT scan?"

Billy Bob nodded, still grinning.

"The doctor said you have a human brain and it works?"

"Yeah! He said I can play. No worries!" Billy

Bob grabbed me and danced me around in a little circle. He stopped abruptly. His eyes grew big as he focused on something behind me. I turned around. Oh, my god. Miss Davis! She was coming down the hall and heading straight at us. She was back in one of her neat, trim suits, but now I knew what was underneath.

She looked around and made sure that no one else was close enough to overhear her. "I just want you to know that I work two nights a week, I'm not a prostitute, and I would appreciate it if you guys didn't say anything."

"We made a pact not to say a word," I assured her. It was true. We figured that given the average teacher's salary, Miss Davis probably needed the extra money. And besides, she put on a rockin' show.

"Thanks," she said, obviously relieved. "Any questions?"

Billy Bob raised his hand. "Will you go to the prom with me?" he asked.

It was the end of our last practice before our last game. Ever. I'd been counting down to this—our final game. But I found myself getting a little sentimental despite myself. This was it for Kilmer's Coyotes. At least for me. And honestly? I wanted to go out in a blaze of glory.

Wanted it bad. Didn't want to go out with my fans writing mean graffiti about me.

We circled up at mid-field around coach Kilmer. "Take a knee!" he commanded. Like an obedient infantry, we all fell to one knee. Kilmer was a bastard, but like Tweeder said, he was our bastard. "It's in your hands," he said. "I promise you that if you come out here tomorrow night and play like you played at Elwood, you will lose big." Me and the strip joint posse traded covert, guilty looks. "And for some of you, tomorrow night will be the last time you'll ever play football," Kilmer went on. Rough stuff. I know more than a few of us felt it in the gut when he said that. "If you follow my game plan, we'll win this thing and go on to the state play-offs. If not, ask yourselves, do you wanna go out losers?" He clapped, like we were breaking huddle. "We're done here. Go on in."

We trooped toward the locker room. Kilmer stopped me before I got inside. "How you feelin,' Johnnie?" He said it almost nicely.

"Alright, I guess," I answered warily.

"You understand that by running the ball we control the clock and we're gonna grind them and the tempo of this game way down. Are you hearing me?"

I was hearing him.

Nice mutated into threatening. "If you disobey me, I will bury you," he said. "I know about the scholarship to Brown and I have your grades under review."

Our bastard? He was *the* bastard of all time. I stared him down. He was not going to get to me.

He gave me an oily smile. "Don't think for a minute that I can't fuck with your transcripts and blow that whole deal for you." His face went tight. "I get what I want. You get what you want."

He was finished. I walked. Quickly. I've said it before, and I'll say it once again. Fuck Kilmer. I couldn't get away from him fast enough.

I let myself into the garage and went straight to the extra fridge for a cold Coke. I grabbed a can, closed the refrigerator door, and popped the tab. I took a long sip as I turned around. I nearly spit it all out as I saw Kyle. He was hanging from the ceiling by one arm, like a monkey. He'd rigged up some kind of harness contraption to hold him, and he'd attached a bizarre assortment of stuff from the garage to his body— a couple of rusty old freeweights, a bicycle pump, a piece of cinderblock, an old leather carpenter's belt stuffed with tools . . . He looked like a hanging garbage dump.

I stared, dumbfounded. He stared back. Well, he wasn't trying to kill himself, or he'd be hanging by his neck. But he was up to something awfully weird. Even for Kyle. Underneath his dangling legs was the knocked over chair he'd used to arrange himself up there.

"God is dead," he said flatly.

"Can I help you down from there?" I asked him. I hadn't figured out why he was up there, but it couldn't be much fun.

Kyle shook his head. "Not yet. I can feel the socket givin' way. Any minute it's gonna dislocate."

"Excuse me? Why are you doin' this?" I was totally mystified. About the arm, about the cult, about everything my little brother did.

"My ankle's healed and Dad's tryin' to make me play football again," Kyle said from up above me, as if it were the most logical explanation in the world.

I started getting this sick feeling in my stomach. I wasn't sure I really wanted to understand what he was telling me. He led me through it. "You remember I broke my ankle?" he asked.

"Yeah."

"Busted it myself. I jumped off the roof."

Busted it himself. Holy shit. His reasoning was just beginning to penetrate, when somehow the harness came loose, and Kyle went crashing to the floor. I rushed over to him. "Kyle? You alright?"

He got up and moved his arm around. "Fuck.

Yeah, shit, I think I'm fine." He wasn't happy about it, either.

"You don't like football?" It wasn't really a question. I finally got it.

"I'm too scared to play," he said. "I'm afraid I'll mess up."

I bit my lower lip. I really got it. Damn. Kyle had been trained to play—just like every other boy in West Canaan. He wasn't bad, either. "Is that what this whole God search has been about?" I asked him. You had to give the kid credit for creativity.

"I guess," Kyle said. He started detaching the weights and tools. "I mean, do you believe that there is a God out there that's gonna watch out for you?"

It was a serious question. I answered it seriously. "I believe there's a force in the universe that people call God or Allah or Jehovah or Buddah or whatever."

"So you believe in God?"

I did believe in . . . something. I tried to explain it. "Remember Miss Haden?"

"The Sunday-school teacher with the mustache?"

I nodded. "She told you the story of the spiteful angels?"

"Probably. I don't remember." Kyle lost the bike pump and the other garbage.

"The angels were jealous when God created people," I recounted.

"Why?"

" 'Cause the angels saw that people could live on earth and feel things and love each other and . . . they were pissed."

"The angels were pissed off."

"Yeah, but then God gave the angels the job of letting people know that God was with them," I said.

"So?" Kyle was still waiting for me to answer his question about God.

"So these pissed off angels hid God where no one ever looks," I said.

"Where?"

I headed for the garage door with my soda. "Inside us somewhere, I guess." It was a nice story. And I think on some level I believed it, too.

The sky was filled with brilliant stars, and was as big as Texas. The air was crisp and clean. It was a beautiful night. With the letter from Brown, my life was as big and open with possibilities as the sky. But I felt that last game hanging over my head—the pressure, the coach's threats. I was high and low all at the same time. I was keyed up about everything. I needed someone to talk to about it, someone to hold me so I knew I'd be okay. And that someone wasn't anyone. That someone was Jules.

She'd avoided me since I'd shown up at Mr. Freeze. And honestly? I hadn't been all that aggressive about tracking her down. It wasn't that I didn't miss her. I did. A lot. And it wasn't that I wasn't thinking about her. I was. Plenty. But I was still pissed that she'd sicced all those fans on me when I was trying to make up with her, and I was hurt that she wasn't even a little happy that I was finally getting some recognition on the field. Of course, after the last game, it wasn't the kind of recognition I needed.

Now I stood on Julie's porch, waiting for her to answer the doorbell. The light went on. She opened the door. She looked absolutely beautiful. Her light brown hair was loose around her shoulders, her face was bare, her skin clear and soft. But her luminous brown eyes had a hard look in them. "What do you want?" she asked guardedly.

"I'm sorry, okay?" She wasn't gonna chase me away this time. "I need to tell you something."

"It's late," she said tonelessly.

"Listen, I got into Brown today. Full academic scholarship."

It took a moment to register. I could see her losing a hold on her anger, despite herself.

"Johnnie, that's great!" She even smiled. "I'm so happy for you."

"But Kilmer's threatening to fuck up my scholarship if I don't play by his rules tomorrow," I said.

The smile faded. "Oh. Wow . . . well, then quit," she said, rationally, matter-of-factly.

"I can't."

"Then play."

I was getting frustrated. "You don't understand."

"You're right. I don't understand," she said.

I took a deep breath. I wasn't gonna get in a thing with Julie again. I needed her on my team tonight. I tried to explain. "If I play for Kilmer tomorrow and we win, *he wins*. And everyone in West Cannan will go on believin' that Bud Kilmer's the greatest coach that ever lived."

"Yeah?" Jules shrugged. Kilmer was just an unpleasant fact of life, was what she was telling me.

"What about the next team he coaches? What if my brother plays for him?" I thought about Kyle, trying to break his own arm so he wouldn't have to be subjected to that. Enough was enough. "I'll be buyin' into everything that's wrong about this town. I love football—when it's pure. But when it's like this . . ."

Jules frowned. "Want some cheese with that whine?"

"What?" I kind of thought I was sticking up for my principles. But Julie saw it differently.

"You're a whiner. Why don't you just step up and play the hero?"

"The hero!" As in go out on that field and kick some butt? I was surprised to hear this from Jules. Surprised and scared. Hard to admit, but true. "Heroes win. What if I lose?" There. It was out. My dirty secret. I was scared shitless. I wasn't so different from Kyle. Okay, I didn't take it quite as far. Who did?

"You're wrong, Mox," Julie said. "Heroes don't always win. It's alright to be scared, but you can't give up outta fear. Or because the coach bullies you. Who cares if you lose? Give absolutely everything and fail. That's the ultimate path of the hero."

I think Julie was telling me to go out there and do my best. Regardless of Coach Bud Kilmer, Sir. But even if I wasn't exactly sure what she was saying, it sounded good. She sounded good. Looked good, too. "Can I come in for a minute?" I asked.

"No, it's late," she said, but she didn't sound angry.

"C'mon. One kiss." I just wanted to be in her arms and forget everything else for a little while.

"My dad's still up. Besides, I only kiss heroes." But her "no" was softened by a genuine smile. I guess she didn't hate me so much anymore. "Get some sleep," she added, with concern.

I returned her smile, and then headed back to the Moxmobile.

13

Maybe it was Julie's smile. I'd gone to bed with it in my mind, slept like a baby, and woken up early, ready to take on—well, if not the world, then at least Gilroy. Now I stood alone in the middle of the football field as the sun rose above the stadium. The white-gold rays came through the bleachers on a slant, crowning the east edge of the field in a corona of light. I sipped coffee from a paper cup, just soaking in the peace and majesty of the morning.

By midafternoon, this place would be jumping. The ground crew would be busy getting the field ready. Concessions would be filling boxes of popcorn and coolers of soft drinks and beer. The local TV stations would be setting up their cameras and equipment. People would be swarming around the stadium entrance, trying to scalp tickets for the sold-out game.

Later still, fans would be charging through the stadium turnstiles, waving blue banners, scrambling for the best seats, raising the noise level in the now silent stadium to a dull roar. Main Street would be a ghost town. "Closed" signs would sprout on the stores like dandelions. The pastor at our church would probably even mention the Coyotes in his early evening service. This was the biggest night of the year in West Canaan. The last game of the season. The only ticket to have tonight. It would be a madhouse here soon enough.

But right now, the place belonged to me. I owned the morning. This moment was mine. I tried to memorize the feeling, to hold on to it. When the stands were full and the opponent was coming at us, I wanted to be able to re-create the power and composure I was feeling now. *For thine is the kingdom, the power and the glory . . .*

"Everything you've done all year means nothing!" Coach Kilmer lectured the circle of players in the locker room. "All those double sessions in the heat mean nothing! All those games we won mean nothing! If you don't win tonight, no district title, and no shot at states. It's up to you! This game is forty-eight minutes for the next forty-eight years of your life!"

I looked around at my teammates. Their faces were drawn with tension and fear. Every nerve in this room was strung tight for battle. I was jittery, too. Then I spied Lance making a silent entrance and joining our circle. The coach barely glanced at him. Lance and I locked gazes. He smiled encouragingly. I knew he was here for us—for the team. Not for Kilmer. Not anymore.

I took a few deep breaths. That's how I was going to play. For us. For the team. Be a hero, Julie had said.

The whole team traded fivers and slaps on the back. We let out a collective roar of "Coyotes!"— a solemn ritual. Then we jogged single-file through the passage to the stadium, and burst out onto the field, tearing right through the huge, long banner the cheering team held up for just this purpose. The banner split in two over-grown ribbons, which the cheerleaders waved through the air. They yelled madly. They spun cartwheels. They raised pom-pommed fists to the night sky.

Across the field, the Gilroy cheering squad was welcoming their own players. Their mascot, a doofy-looking fake cowboy on a real horse, galloped on the sidelines. The opposition streamed on from the away-team entrance. They were pumped, they were huge, they were . . . as nervous and determined as we were. Fans from both sides roared with anticipation.

I looked up in the stands to where I knew my family would be. Mom, Dad and Kyle were all on their feet. The Harbors were right next to them. With Julie. Yup, even Jules was stoked for the final game. I thought about her smile, and the feeling I'd had right in this very spot this morning. I inhaled deeply. I breathed out. I was ready.

I faced down the Gilroy quarterback at midfield for the opening coin toss. His expression behind his helmet was as taut as mine. We reached out and shook hands. Who knows—under different circumstances we might have been buds. On any other day we might have drunk a beer together and talked about the Cowboys. But this was the guy whose team we were gonna take down, no matter how violently. This was the guy who wasn't even gonna lead his team past the 50-yard line, let alone into the end zone.

"Heads," I said.

The ref made the toss. I held my breath for a moment. "Heads it is."

Yes! The first victory. Luck was with us. I elected to receive. The Gilroy Q.B. walked away, his coach already yelling like the lost toss was his fault.

Game time. This was it. Gilroy boomed the opening kickoff high into the floodlit sky. I watched the pigskin soar through the air. Johnson grabbed it cleanly at the 2, and finessed his way through the massive Gilroy bruisers to the 40-yard line. Good man! I pumped my fist. An excellent run to start us in prime field position. The Coyote crowd cheered wildly.

As I started moving onto the field with my offense, Kilmer grabbed me by the arm. "Remember what I said," he growled. "Now go fetch me a championship!"

I was gonna fetch it. But not for him. I sprinted onto the field and huddled with my teammates. We were pumped. I could see it in everyone's eyes. We broke huddle and lined up. Billy Bob was three-hundred something pounds of rage. He snorted and growled and kicked turf. The Gilroy D had reason to be scared. They winced and fidgeted as we faced off at the line of scrimmage.

Billy Bob let out a fiercesome bellow as I took the snap from center. I handed the ball off crisply to Wendell. He found a clean hole and charged up the middle. I watched him go, go . . . yes! A twelve yard gain. We were gonna be unstoppable. I could feel it.

The Wendell show continued from there. He was amazing. He found an opening on the left side and scampered 20 yards to the 28. The next thing you knew he was carrying three Mustang linemen inside the 10.

The home crowd was going insane. Wendell was on fire as always, and I was grateful.

I would have been a lot more ecstatic, however, if I'd had anything to do with it, really. The problem was that Kilmer was shuttling in every play. After that first play I'd called, I was a mere hand-off machine, and I was starting to feel a little useless here. I shot Kilmer an angry look. He didn't so much as glance back. I was starting to lose hold of my optimistic mood. Somehow Kilmer made me feel like a second string again. I doubt he would have called it this way with Lance still in the game.

Next down, and Wilkes, a red-haired junior, came in with the play. "Split thirty-five dive slot left," the fullback said.

I saw Wendell turn away in disgust. You couldn't blame him. The guy had run the hell out of that ball all the way from the 40, and now that we were in scoring range, Kilmer was giving it away to the white guy. I knew exactly how Wendell felt. The coach was stealing this game from us. We were pawns to be used and thrown away.

I made a snap decision. *I* was the quarterback. It was time for *me* to start calling the plays, and I was gonna give Wendell some of his due glory. "Let's change that to split twenty-five dive slot left," I said. I grinned at Wendell. "I'll get you in the end zone."

The guys in the huddle looked at me warily. I'd made a bold call, changing Kilmer's play. "What? Somebody have a problem with Wendell puttin' one in the end zone?" I asked. Damn. We'd see just who was in charge around here. Suddenly, I was back in the game—and it felt good.

My teammates were with me.

"Got it!"

"Sweep for Wendell."

"Okay, Mox!" they chimed in.

Wendell was grinning as the huddle broke. The snap. The hand-off. Smooth as silk. Wendell plowed in for a touchdown. He was there! He was in! We plowed in after him. He leapt on top of me. We slapped and patted and hollered with triumph.

"Wen-dell! Wen-dell!" Darcy and the cheerleaders chanted his name. Our fans chanted along.

But the coach was stone-faced. Pissed about how we'd changed the play. So what? After the extra point conversion, we were up 7-zip. He shoulda been pissing-in-pants happy.

But a few minutes later, I watched helplessly as the Gilroy halfback broke down the sideline and ran 50 yards for a touchdown—practically untouched by our defense.

Dammit! They'd evened the score. That was too fast. Now it was really time to get back to business. We took the field and on the first snap from center Wendell found a huge gap and squirted up the middle with the ball. The end zone was in clear reach.

Suddenly, I saw Wendell grab his calf. Some whack muscle spasm or something. Next thing, a Gilroy linebacker closed the distance between them, and delivered a catastrophic crash. I winced as Wendell went down. I could see him holding that calf with both hands, and writhing in pain. The ball was rolling free. Gilroy pounced on the fumble and recovered it.

The Coyote fans were on their feet, but silent, all worried eyes on Wendell. I raced over to him. Two trainers sprinted across the field to his aid. Out of the corner of my eye, I saw Billy Bob shove the linebacker who'd made the hit.

I pulled off my helmet and knelt beside Wendell. Even the gentlest probing of his leg by the trainers was sending him into silent spasms of pain. Coach Bates was there too, shaking his head.

Kilmer approached. "He tore something," Coach Bates informed him grimly.

"Can you fix him?" Coming from Kilmer, that was more of an order than a question.

Anger welled up in me. Fix him? The way he'd fixed Lance? Helplessly, I watched as Wendell draped his arms around the trainers and Coach Bates shepherded them off the field. I couldn't catch Wendell's eye. I wanted to run after him and yell for him not to let them mess around with his leg. But the ref blew his whistle, signaling play to resume.

With Wendell out and our spirit out with him, Gilroy took control of the game. Before we knew it, their Q.B. whizzed an awesome spiral through the air, and the wide receiver nabbed it cleanly. Touchdown, Gilroy. And suddenly we were down by 7.

It got even worse as I took the field with our Wendell-less offense. Kilmer was sending in the same old plays, but Wilkes was running them instead. I didn't quite see how we were gonna score when Wilkes was losing yardage every time I gave him the ball.

Nothing against the guy, but he wasn't Wendell. Soon it was third and nine and the coach was shuttling in another bozo play. Another hand-off to Wilkes. No way that was gonna get us a first down. As it turned out, I barely had the snap from center in my hands when I was tasting huge chunks of dirt. A pile of Gilroy meatheads were on top of me in a nanosecond, reducing my body to a crumpled mess. A shooting pain went through my shoulder. One hip throbbed. I managed to limp to the sidelines.

"Third and nine," Lance said to me on the bench. "You gotta throw the ball." The mood on the West Canaan side was lower than a sunken battleship.

I was tense with frustration. "Kilmer keeps stickin' to the same game plan, even with Wendell down," I bitched.

"You could throw on these guys, Mox," Lance said. "You just gotta do it on first down."

Of course Lance was right, but it was easy for him to say. He was no longer one of Coach Bud Kilmer's faithful subjects. When his star had fallen, he'd toppled free of Kilmer's rules and commands.

Not so for me. I put my helmet on and moved toward the field. Kilmer stopped me. "Kneel on it," he ordered me.

"What? There's a minute left, let me throw a few," I protested.

"I'm not taking any chances. Run the clock out," the coach said. In the Days of Lance, the coach would definitely have bet on him to throw. This was a vote of no confidence for me.

This was the coach telling me I couldn't do it. That he wouldn't let me try.

A wave of futility crashed over me. Why was I trying to fight it? Why not take the path of least resistance, and just wait for it to be over? Like a blade of grass bending in a windstorm so it didn't break.

It was humiliating enough running onto the field and ending the half by kneeling on the ball. But the hometown crowd booing their displeasure made me wish I'd never put on a uniform. Finally, the gun went off. Halftime. If only the game were over already.

I peered into the trainer's room and I thought I was having déjà vu. You know, when you've seen it happen before? It was just like with Lance. Except it was Wendell sitting up there on the table. And it was his calf—his Achilles tendon, to be exact—and not his knee. But there was the trainer, filling a syringe, and there was Coach Kilmer overseeing the whole process. Coach Bates was in there, too. I heard him encouraging Wendell. "You're a gamer, Wendell."

I took a step into the room. "Wendell? What are you doin'?"

It was Kilmer who answered. "He's gettin' back in the game."

Suddenly, Tweeder was next to me. "I heard the pop, Wendell. It's a tendon."

"Don't do this," I added.

"Get outta here, both of you!" Kilmer's voice was low and threatening. "You two wouldn't know anything about dedication and team play."

"But I would!" I whirled around. Lance! He hobbled toward us on his crutches. "Don't do it, Wendell. Don't throw away your career for Kilmer. It's not worth it."

Coach Kilmer laughed—a mean, harsh sound. "You gonna listen to that? Comin' from a gimp who's prayin' for us to lose so he can feel like the missing link? Forget it. Give him the shot."

The trainer held the needle up. Coach Bates swabbed Wendell's calf with alcohol. My pulse beat with anger and defeat.

"Wait!" It was Billy Bob. He squeezed through the doorframe, into the tiny and crowded trainer's room. He was covered with mud and sweat. We all were. "You put that shot anywhere near Wendell's leg, and I swear on my mama's grave that I'll tear your arms out and beat you to death with them." His words rang with the force and pain of Kilmer's ridicule.

"Billy Bob, this has got nothing to do with you," Coach Kilmer told him.

"No, it has to do with all of us," I said. I

motioned to the sea of frustrated players sitting on the locker room benches or standing and listening to us. By now, we had everyone's attention. "We've killed ourselves for you. We've played hurt and sick. We spend most of the time so fuckin' scared we're gonna do somethin' wrong, and you'll kick our ass. No, it's not about Billy Bob or me . . . but it's not about you, either."

Kilmer looked at me for a very long second. Then he turned to the trainer. "Give 'im the shot."

"No!" I went right up to the coach's leathery, mean face. "You give him that shot and I quit. Find another quarterback."

Kilmer thought I was bluffing. "You ready to blow your future?"

"The scholarship? Fuck it! Take it! You can have it! If it keeps the needle outta his leg and lets me sleep at night, you can have it. I don't give a fuck. I'm out." I was raging and scared. But what else could I do? Suck up to Kilmer and protect my butt by sacrificing Wendell's? Was that what this game was all about? Trading on your friends and teammates? Was that what playing together was all about?

Kilmer pushed me away and stepped toward Tweeder. "Tweeder, you'll take the snaps and—"

"Fuck you. I'm out, too," Tweeder said. He

moved toward me. So did Billy Bob. And Lance. I wanted to cheer.

And Kilmer wanted to throttle me. He lunged at me and grabbed my jersey. I froze. I really thought he was going to hurt me good.

But out in the main part of the locker room, the Coyote players were mobilizing. They pushed toward us. They surrounded us. Kilmer let go of me and faced the mob. "All of you!" he thundered. "Put your helmets on and take the field! Now!"

No one moved. Oh, my god, this was great. It was mutiny. Sweet revenge. "The only way we're goin' back out there is without you," I said. I could feel it again—that power and composure I'd found this morning. And this time, I had forty-strong players behind me to boot.

Kilmer struggled to turn it around. "I love you, boys." He was all sticky emotion now. His voice was cloying. "I would never do anything to hurt any one of yas. You know that. Lord strike me down if I did." The coward—using God's name to bend us to his will. "You know I'd lay down for yas anytime, anywhere," he went on. "You're like my sons, and I'm walking out that door and I'm askin' you to trust me. Follow me."

He walked out, the sea of players parting to let him through. Coach Bates hurried after him.

The lap dog. But none of the rest of us moved. We watched the two of them cross the locker room. They stepped into the tunnel that led to the stadium. The door slammed behind them.

You could have heard that proverbial pin drop in the locker room. We were all shocked silent. Kilmer had been a brutal fact of life for so long that it was hard to get our minds around the fact that he was finished. That we'd finished him. He was out there. We were in here. His reign was over. We were free. Most of us had dreamed this moment, imagined it. I know I had. But doing it—taking down the West Canaan icon for real—I hadn't thought it possible until the second we'd actually done it.

The whole team gaped at me—part incredulity, part admiration, part fear. I could see it all in their wide-eyed expressions. We were free—but we were also sailing without a captain, if you know what I mean. We'd been taking orders from Kilmer automatically all these years. Now who was gonna steer the ship?

The locker room door swung open. I think we all expected to see Kilmer again. But a ref stepped in, black and white striped shirt, whistle around his neck. "Let's go, fellas. If you're gonna warm up, you should do that now." He stepped back out.

Everyone was still looking at me. Well, I guess

it was only natural, since I'd led the mutiny. I clapped to get the energy flowing. "Okay, let's do this!"

They all stared at me. Right. I guess it was easier said than done.

I thought fast. "I'll call the plays from the line . . ." I looked at Lance. "And Lance will coach the game from the sidelines."

They kept staring at me. From the looks on their faces, you'd think I'd just given them driving directions to their own funerals. I had to rally the troops. I thought about what Julie had said the night before. "What? We shouldn't be scared," I said. "We're already gettin' our asses kicked. Kilmer said, 'forty-eight minutes for the next forty-eight years of our lives.' Fuck that. Let's play twenty-four minutes for the next twenty-four minutes and leave it on the field. We got the rest of our lives to be mediocre, but we can play like gods for the next twenty-four minutes. We can't be afraid to lose."

Can't be afraid to lose. That's what Julie had said, and now I really understood it. If you weren't afraid to lose, you wouldn't be afraid to win, either. "The ultimate path of the hero is to give absolutely everything and fail," I said, borrowing her lines. Hell, they'd worked for me, why not for my team? "If we go out there and half-ass it 'cause we're scared? And we lose?

We'll always wonder what would have happened if we gave it everything. If we give
absolutely everything and we lose . . . that's
heroic. Let's be heroes."

I thought it was a decent speech. Billy Bob
added the necessary final punch. "AAAaaaahh-
hhhh!" he yelled like an animal.

"AAAaaahhhhh!" Everyone joined in. We
raised our helmets, sounding our brute cries, as
we exploded out of the locker room, through the
tunnel and onto the field. Or should I say, onto
our field?

"I need five wide receivers," Lance said. His
voice was confident, in control. He sounded like
a general who'd been giving orders to his troops
all his life. "We're running the Oop-de-Oop." I
grinned. The good old Oop-de-Oop. Good for
Lance. "No running backs. No tight ends. I want
four receivers stacked left, Tweeder on the right.
We overload their left side, and force them to
cover Tweeder one on one."

"Mano a mano," Tweeder said, stoked.

"And *no* huddles," I added.

Billy Bob's eyes opened wide. "Say what?"

"Kilmer got us in better shape than Gilroy," I
explained. All those early morning killer work-
outs had to be good for something. We'd go
without stopping. Run those suckers from

Gilroy right into the turf. "I'll call plays on the line," I told Billy Bob. "Defense won't know what hit 'em."

Up in the stands, the crowd was confused. You could see 'em looking all over—for the coach. My folks and Kyle were in their spot, looking around, too. "Where the hell is he?" they were asking each other right about now. Maybe some fans were checking out Lance, and getting wise to who was calling the game. Others weren't bothering to figure it out. We'd been losing a steady trickle of the nonbelievers since Wendell had gone down. No matter. That was about to change.

On the field, the opponent was confused, too. The Oop-de-Oop was way excellent for that. Our team was lined up in whack formation. Gilroy couldn't figure out what we were up to. I saw a couple of their players counting receivers on their fingers, and wondering how the hell they were gonna cover them.

On the sidelines, the refs were counting on their fingers, too.

"Thirty-four, twnety-two, Red Jimmy, seventy-nine, hut, hut—" I barked. I took the snap and faded back. To my left, the sea of Coyote receivers sprinted downfield. Gilroy's linebackers were flooded. I spotted Johnson wide open by the sidelines, and uncorked a bullet that landed in his gut. The completion was good for 16 yards and a first down.

The trickle of fans out the exit stopped. We had their full attention. We lined up immediately and caught Gilroy totally off guard. They were still stuck in the their huddle as I called a quick count. I took the snap, stepped back, and hit Tweeder over the middle. Good for 21 yards!

On the sidelines, the down marker officials couldn't move the sticks fast enough. Without stopping to huddle, we were making too many first downs for them to keep up. I saw a ref trip over the chains. I liked it. I loved it. My confidence swelled. The fans loved it, too. My family, Jules . . . the whole town was watching me. We kept throwing, catching, running. One down marker official wiped the sweat off his brow with the back of his sleeve.

And the Gilroy players were even more wiped out. The game plan was working perfectly. I called another quick snap and it was like taking candy from a baby. There wasn't a defender within 15 yards of Johnson, who was all alone in the end zone, waiting for the ball. All I had to do was let him have it.

Touchdown!!

Nii-iice! I slapped fives with Billy Bob. We went into a wild end zone dance.

The Gilroy D was finished. One of their linebackers fell right onto the turf on his huge butt. The down-marker officials threw the chains on the ground in relief. The fans were on their feet, cheering, stamping, whistling. The cheerleaders were literally head over heels.

We staggered to the sidelines, out of breath and exhausted, but busting with pride. We'd evened the score. It was 14-all. Billy Bob hit the oxygen tank like a drunk hitting an open bar. The rest of us just hit the ground in various sitting or lying down positions. I closed my eyes for a moment and tried to will my racing pulse to slow down.

"Stand up! Stand up!" Lance rallied us, tough but encouraging. "I know you're tired, but you don't have to show them that. You're playin' the game of your lives!" he exclaimed.

It was true, and I knew it. We were playin' with everything we had, and it was working. The pride gave me just enough energy to get myself back up. Lance was a hundred percent right. "Stand proud!" he regaled us. "You want them to think we're beat?"

That did it. "No way!" our offense chorused, getting back onto their feet.

"Let 'em see that we're in this!" Lance thundered.

The Coyotes revived with cheers and hand

slaps. We stood proudly, and watched our D try to hold the Gilroy line.

But they managed to move their ball into our territory, and suddenly they were lining up for a field goal attempt. The Gilroy kicker's 27-yarder split the uprights. Damn! We were losing again. As we all glanced up at the clock, we saw there were only 7 minutes, 7 seconds left in the game.

"Don't sweat it, guys," Lance said intensely. "Just focus. We can still win this game."

I tried to heed his words. Focus. Power, composure. Back on the field we were running our no huddle offense again. It seemed to be our best weapon. I looked to Lance for his signal. This was our moment. We had to take the game now. He did this weird twisty motion with one hand, and pummeled it with his other hand. Huh? Was it a button hook left, or fly right? I wasn't sure what play he was calling.

He signaled again. I turned my palms up to show him I couldn't read it. He did the signal a third time, but I still didn't get it.

"Time out! Mox, call a time out!" he yelled.

Time out? But we'd gained ground by playing Gilroy into the turf, by wearing them out, by not stopping. And that was how we were going to win this thing. It was now or never. I waved off Lance's request and called a play. I took the snap, rolled out to the left, and heaved the ball at a pack of four Coyote receivers. But a Gilroy defender leapt into their midst and intercepted it.

I was furious at myself. I shoulda called time out like Lance had wanted. I shook my head hard as I headed to the sidelines. There wasn't enough time left for a mistake like that. What if I'd just lost us the whole damned game?

Lance came forward to meet me. "You gotta listen to me," he said. "Shake that off. Let it go, now." Let it go? I looked at him. "Just listen to me. Keep your head in the game now." He somehow managed to reproach and inspire me at the same time. I felt a new admiration for him. The guy was good.

On the field, Gilroy ran a trap up the middle. BOOM! We stopped them cold. But they were only a foot away from a first down and we were in trouble. Critical trouble. We were out of time outs and losing 17–14. There were only 38 seconds left in the game. If Gilroy made another first down, they could run out the clock.

On the side, Lance and I traded grim looks. "They're going for it," I said. "We don't stop 'em here, it's the game."

Billy Bob staggered up to us. His uniform was soaked and bloody. He grabbed Lance by the shoulders. "I'll stop 'em!" he roared, his eyes gleaming wildly.

"You wanna play defense?" Lance asked warily.

"Put me in. I'll stop 'em," Billy Bob responded.

Lance thought for a moment. He nodded. Billy Bob charged out on the field, tapped Linehan, a bulky lineman, on the shoulder and assumed his position.

As Linehan trotted in, I turned to Lance with awe and respect. It was a crazy move. It was a daring move. But it might work. "Putting him in there is insane," I said. "*I love it!* . . . but it's insane." Then again, it might not work.

Darcy led the cheering squad in a rousing cry of "Hold that line!" I don't think there was a single Coyote fan who wasn't on his or her feet. I held my breath as Billy Bob crouched on the line. He let out an industrial strength belch that I could hear even from the sideline.

Gilroy took the snap. We could see their fullback leaping into the air to try and take that final yard. I didn't know the B-meister could move his huge body so fast. I'd never seen him do anything like it before. Billy Bob got under that fullback, and plucked him right out of the goddamn sky. Hey, anything can happen in football, and tonight it did. He had the Gilroy fullback in his arms. He hurled him back at the Gilroy Q.B. like a sack of potatoes. I swear to you. Billy Bob really did that.

Our fans were out of their minds. They drove their fists into the air. They shouted. "Coyotes take possession at the Coyote forty-two," the P.A. system squawked.

I ran out onto the field with the rest of my unit, and we mobbed Billy Bob, hooting and cheering for him. I hugged him like an oversized teddy bear. High on his incredible play, we huddled up. It was up to me again, and to the Coyote offense. Billy Bob had stopped Gilroy in their tracks. But we still had to score. I took a deep breath. Composure. Power. "Z-out, sideline flash, on three, make sure you get outta bounds and stop the clock," I said.

We had 27 seconds left to score.

The second I got that damn ball in my hands, I rolled out like I was escaping from a blazing house. I scrambled and fired an eight-yard pass to Tweeder. I watched him fighting to get out of bounds, but he didn't make it. The clock was running. 18, 17, 16 . . . I counted the seconds in my head and grimaced as the Gilroy defense dragged their feet lining up. Their mascot reared up on its hind legs, as the fake cowboy pantomimed a slow defense.

I led a charge toward the new line of scrimmage. As soon as I got the snap, I hurled the ball out of bounds—and nailed the fake cowboy. He flew off his horse and crumpled to the ground.

Okay. I'd killed two birds—or mustangs—with one stone. Nailed their mascot and stopped the clock, too. Now we had 7 seconds left to score.

This was it. Our final huddle. Our last chance. I looked at Lance and we communicated with hand signals. I had a daring—but possibly brilliant idea. I signaled it to Lance. I could see he was surprised. But a second later he signaled me to go ahead. I called the play. I could see how astonished everyone was. Especially Billy Bob.

"Aw, no, not that lame-ass play where I pretend I'm lost?"

I nodded and our offense lined up. We had four receivers stacked in twos on the left, but none on the right. Except for Billy Bob—the biggest, fattest tight end the gridiron had ever seen. Fulson, our refrigerator-sized fullback, lined up behind me.

The cheerleaders screamed for a touchdown. The fans stomped their feet. Lance paced the sidelines like Lou Holtz in the Orange Bowl.

I practically had my fingers crossed as I took the snap. It was a risky play, and I knew it. But nothing ventured, nothing gained, as they say. Especially at a critical moment like this. I handed off to Fulson and led him around the left side.

Tweeder swept across the backfield, and took

the ball on a reverse. Yes! I liked the way he sucked that baby up! He ran right. Everyone was on him. Meanwhile, Billy Bob was staggering around downfield, looking completely lost. No one even bothered to pick him up. Tweeder stopped short at the line of scrimmage, and before Gilroy had a split second to get wise, he hurled the pigskin right to me. I got my hands on it and looked downfield.

Shit! Billy Bob hadn't turned around! Damn! I was stuck with the ball—just like I'd been during that hungover excuse for a game against Elwood. The Mustang defenders were closing in on me. I had to scramble. Right, left. I got free. Billy Bob finally turned around. I threw immediately. It soared. It was a beaut. I held my breath. I almost couldn't stand to watch.

And he got it! Billy Bob grabbed it inside the ten yard line! Yesss! Go, Billy Bob! Put that sucker into the end zone! But something was wrong. He wasn't moving. He just stood there waving the ball in the air. Oh, my god, I just wasn't seeing this! Billy Bob was so excited and amazed at sucking in that ball, that he was forgetting to run with it.

He swiveled his helmeted head, looking around him. A Gilroy lineman was racing right toward him. Billy Bob suddenly seemed to wake up. He drove a ferocious straight-arm into the guy's middle, and trotted comfortably across the 5 yard line. But two safeties were bearing down on him. One—two—boom—boom! He flattened both of them like silly putty. A trio of defenders grabbed his legs. But the man was our very own King Kong, our Godzilla, our doughy, meat-headed Superman. He dragged them across the 4 and kept going.

The entire Gilroy D was charging him now, seizing his arms, jumping on his back. As I ran toward him, Billy Bob's blue and white uniform was barely visible under a swarming mountain of Mustang gold. But the mountain kept moving. Some of our offense piled up to push Billy Bob from behind. He was over the 3, the 2 . . . This was the most outrageous, incredible spectacle I'd ever witnessed on the field!

From under the mountain of Gilroy gold, Billy Bob let out a roar. "AAAAAAAHHHHHH-HHHHH!" The noise and vibrations shook his tacklers. Someone fell off the pile. Someone else stumbled. And Billy Bob himself was toppling over, bringing the rest of the mountain down with him . . . down, down . . . Oh, my god! Sweet heaven—the guy was falling right into the end zone!

TOUCHDOWN!! The gun went off.

I had one stunned, incredulous, paralyzed moment. I couldn't have just seen that happen.

But it *had* happened. Billy Bob had scored the winning touchdown! We'd done it! We were champs!

The realization hit me. Triumph surged through my body. I let out the mother of all Coyote howls as I raced toward Billy Bob in the end zone. The fans erupted in delirium. The stands emptied of West Canaan spectators as they all poured onto the field. I got through to Billy Bob and grabbed him. We both howled. I took his hands and we spun around like two little kids.

And then my dad was hugging me and Mom and Kyle. The P.A. system crackled with electricity as they announced our victory, but the noise in the end zone almost drowned it out.

I caught sight of Wendell charging through the madness as if he were plowing through the offense—and he had Julie with him, smiling, radiant. Jules! I held her gaze as I went toward her, and the crowd just parted like the Red Sea for us. I pulled her up into my arms.

"Wendell told me what you did!" she yelled over the noise of the crowd. She took my face in her hands and pulled me close. Our mouths were only inches apart. I looked into her shining brown eyes. "I thought you only kissed heroes," I said.

Our lips met. We kissed long and deep, as if we were the only people on the field. I could feel my heart beating against her. I drank in her sweetness and—what the . . . !? Suddenly, beer was spilling on our heads and down our faces. We pulled apart, shrieking and laughing as Tweeder poured out the rest of the bottle. The official celebration had begun. And as I think you know by now, we're pretty damned good at celebrating in West Canaan.

Billy Bob cried because he's a bit of a crier, and Tweeder drank beers because Tweeder drinks beer. Lance was content. He may have found his calling as a football coach. Wendell will get his ride to Grambling. And me? I was happy. The day was ours and no one can ever take it away.

So for some of us, maybe it ends without us knowing it. Maybe these are the last days, and I'll never play football again. I don't know if it had anything to do with the pissed-off angels or the ultimate path of the hero, but I will never forget this day.